THE STOWAWAY

THE STOWAWAY

Hope you enjoy.

Mike Simmons

Mike Simmons

Matador
9 Priory Business Park,
Wistow Road,
Kibworth Beauchamp
Leicester LE8 0RX, UK
Tel: (+44) 116 279 2299
Fax: (+44) 116 279 2277
Email: books@troubador.co.uk
Web: www.troubador.co.uk/matador

ISBN 978 1848767 393

British Library Cataloguing in Publication Data.
A catalogue record for this book is available from the British Library.

Typeset in 11.5pt Book Antiqua by Troubador Publishing Ltd, Leicester, UK

Matador is an imprint of Troubador Publishing Ltd

Printed and bound in the UK by TJ International, Padstow, Cornwall

To Tim Wood, who the author and a youth group took their first narrowboat trip with many years ago, on a memorable week's journey from Bull's Bridge to Hemel Hempstead and back.

To my ever diligent editor and proof reader Helen Jones

CONTENTS

CHAPTER ONE:

Peggy and Tim

It was Peggy's birthday. She was 60 years old. Peggy was quite a large, round sort of person, with apple-red cheeks, who always seemed to be very cheerful and jolly. From the window of her small flat above the butcher shop, she could see the canal as it passed by the meadow. This is where her little narrow boat,

1

"Turtle", had been moored when it had caught fire. The people of the village had been very kind to her, in particular the butcher, Mr Strout, who had loaned her the flat, complete with all the furniture. But she missed living on board Turtle terribly. She had owned the little boat for 20 years and had taken it on many trips along the canals and rivers of England.

She didn't remember much about the fire that could have caused her so much harm. It had been a cold winter's evening and she remembered putting more coal on the stove, then sitting down to read a book. The next thing she knew was lying on the towpath with Rocket Ron, who moored his boat near the boatyard, kneeling next to her. They couldn't get the fire engine any nearer than the canal shop car park, so the firemen had run down the towpath with a big pump, hoses and fire extinguishers. Using the water from the canal, it had seemed to take ages to put the fire out. Rocket Ron told her later that he had just returned from walking his two ferrets Frankie and Freddie. He had seen smoke coming from the windows of the boat and banged on the door. When he got no reply, he pushed it open and found Peggy slumped in the chair and the boat full of flames and smoke. Pulling her out, he laid her on the towpath and telephoned the fire brigade and ambulance on his mobile phone. The boat was completely destroyed, along with all of Peggy's belongings and memories. She was kept in hospital overnight and then stayed with her friend Trip Boat Tim in his cottage for four weeks before moving to the flat in the village.

. She reached out and touched the wooden sign that was screwed to the wall in her sitting room; it was Turtle's wooden name-plate. Tim had rescued it before British Waterways had taken the boat away to be scrapped. Carefully, he had cleaned and varnished it and then returned it to Peggy.

Every day she touched the sign and promised herself that she and a new Turtle would one day be afloat on the canal again.

Tim, Rocket Ron, Jean Lovell from the canal shop and Harry Martin, who ran the boat hire company, had invited Peggy to lunch in The Barge restaurant on the canal. As it was her birthday, she would wear her special straw hat and green flowery dress, and her favourite leather sandals. Before leaving for The Barge, she tidied away her paints and brushes and stood a finished painted teapot by the window to dry in the sun. Peggy had been interested in canal art ever since she was a young girl. This was the traditional paintwork of canal boats. In the corner of the room she had a big box full of plain teapots, vases, and two Buckby cans all waiting to be painted. When she was finished, they would be sold in the little canal shop by the lock.

Peggy left her little flat in the village and walked to the churchyard, where the footpath led across the meadow to the canal. She could hear the children from St. Mark's Primary School, whose playground was just beyond the tall trees. Often Mrs. Phillips, the head teacher, would ask Peggy to visit the school and show the children how to paint roses and castles onto paper plates. Some were very good indeed, and were displayed in the school hall on parents' evening.

Crossing over the double wooden lock gate she passed Tim's white cottage and the little canal shop with its small flower garden. Although the front of The Barge restaurant was on Springwell Lane, its back garden reached right down to the side of the canal. There were moorings at the bottom for six boats and the boat owners would stop here in the summer and sit in the garden at the tables under the large red umbrellas. There were some swings, a roundabout and a seesaw for their children to play on. Next to the garden was a field where people would camp in tents or stay in caravans.

Trip Boat Tim, Jean, Rocket Ron and Harry were all sitting at a large table by the window overlooking the garden. They sang "Happy Birthday" to Peggy as she came into the room, and then Rocket Ron gave Peggy a birthday card signed by them all and another envelope.

"Oh how lovely," she said, when she had opened it, "tickets to the circus!"

"We're all coming with you," said Tim, "Saturday evening. Is that OK?"

"That's great," said Peggy with a smile, "really great."

They enjoyed a very nice birthday lunch of steak and chips with apple pie and cream, and then late in the afternoon went back to Tim's cottage for a cup of tea and a piece of the birthday cake that Jean Lovell had made.

"By the way, Peggy," said Harry Martin, "I was going to ask you a favour."

"I thought there was a catch to the lunch," she said, laughing.

"No, you'll enjoy this. One of my boats has to go into the dry dock to have some welding repairs done on the hull and the nearest is Boswell's Yard – three days away. I thought you might like to...." Tim interrupted. "Of course she will."

"Thank you," said Peggy, punching Tim on the arm. "I can answer for myself. I'd love to. Be nice to be steering a boat again."

"That's what I thought," Harry smiled.

Walking back across the meadow that evening, Peggy thought how lucky she was to have such good friends. She was looking forward to her journey on the canal.

The circus came every summer. On a field at the edge of the village, they would put up a tall white big top tent and surround it with brightly coloured caravans and trailers. At night, it was lit up like a Christmas tree. There was also a small fairground

5

with dodgem cars, rides and side stalls. Peggy always thought how much circus people were like boaters – they were constant travellers who were always on the move. As well as the many people who came to the circus from the surrounding villages, it was also an annual event for boating people and the moorings on both sides of the canal would be full up all week. Peggy remembered the excitement when some years ago, a chimpanzee called Charlie had escaped and climbed up the long guy ropes that held the big tent in place. Charlie stayed on the roof of the big top for a long time and only came down when he got hungry, just like his trainer had said he would.

On Saturday evening, Peggy met the others at the entrance to the field where a brightly lit sign above a tall archway read, "Welcome to the Circus." A young boy of about 11 with bright ginger hair was selling programmes. Peggy thought he looked very grubby and could do with a good meal.

"Programme, lady?" he called as Peggy passed.

She smiled, gave him two pounds and took one. As they walked towards the big top, she heard a man's voice. It was loud and angry.

"You had better sell all of those, kid – earn your keep."

Peggy looked back to see the young boy and a rough looking man in a scruffy jacket with long, untidy hair. The boy was clearly frightened of the man and he started shouting more loudly.

"Programmes, programmes, buy a programme – only two pounds."

Tim, seeing Peggy's concern, touched her on the arm.

"Leave it, Peggy. It's nothing to do with us."

There were no wild animals used in the circus acts any more, although Peggy could still remember when there were lions and tigers and African elephants. The crowds still loved it, though, as the trapeze artists flew through the air, just catching each other in time, and jugglers threw flaming sticks to each other, and people always jumped at the loud bang from the human cannonball, even though they knew it would make a noise. But it was the clowns that Peggy liked – their brightly coloured clothes and painted faces. She would have loved to have been a clown and make people laugh, although she knew that all clowns have a sad side. During the interval, they saw the young boy again. He was sweeping up in the ring after the riders on horseback had finished performing. He looked up and saw Peggy. She gave him a little wave, and he smiled.

After the final act had finished, they walked around the little fairground that was next to the big top tent. Tim had always fancied himself as a marksman, so he challenged Rocket Ron, an ex-soldier, to a match on the air rifle stall. Rocket Ron won. Tim blamed the sights on the rifle. The loser had to buy the toffee apples. They made their way back to the village, stopping off at The Red Lion pub for a drink.

"OK," said Harry. "I'll see you at the boatyard on Monday, then, Peggy."

"See you then," said Peggy. "And see you tomorrow, Jean. Thank you all for a lovely evening."

On Thursdays and Fridays, Peggy worked with Jean in the little canal shop. Jean and Peggy had been friends for many years. They had met when they were both youngsters at the St. Mark's Church youth club. Neither of them had lived in the village as girls, and would travel from their homes in the surrounding villages to the club. Eventually, they both became Youth Leaders and spent many happy years taking the youngsters on all different types of activities. They would also organise weekend canoe journeys along the canal, camping overnight in a farmer's field. Peggy enjoyed meeting the passing boat people that came into the shop, especially the ones that hired boats from Harry Martin. They always seemed so happy and wanted to know all about the canals. She would help them with the lock by Tim's cottage, showing them how to let the water in and out, and how to use the ropes on the bow and stern of the boat. Many of them would also want to know which route to take and how far they could travel in a day. Peggy would explain that the speed limit was just four miles an hour, and when they went through a lock, it could take as long as travelling a whole mile, especially in the summer when there were a lot of boats on the canal.

Peggy arrived at Harry's boatyard at 9 o'clock on Monday morning. Harry was in his office.

"Morning Harry," she said. "Reporting for service, just show me the boat and I'll be off."

Harry and Peggy walked to the end of a line of moored boats until they reached a blue and white narrowboat called 'Kingfisher'. Harry passed her the keys.

"I'll leave you to it, then," he said. "Ring me if there are any problems."

Peggy dropped her bag onto a bunk in the stern cabin and then lifted up the engine cover. She looked down the right hand side of the engine and pulled out the long metal dipstick, so she could check the oil level. Then she turned the pressure cap on top of the radiator to check the water level in the engine. Finally, she put the long, polished brass tiller bar and pin onto the tiller, so she would be able to steer the boat. When she turned the ignition key, the diesel engine gave a little cough and then burst into life. A puff of grey smoke came from the exhaust pipe. Peggy stood with her hand on the tiller bar and the engine throbbing beneath her feet. "Now I feel at home," she said to herself.

Taking the mid line that was attached to the roof of the boat, she took the end of the rope near to the stern, where she was standing, so she could reach it.

This would be very important, as she was working the boat on her own, and needed to be able to jump on and off the boat with the line in her hand. She untied the lines at the front and back of the boat, pushed off from the jetty, gave the throttle a little burst of power and she was under way.

Peggy turned left out of the boatyard and headed towards the lock. It was only a mile away, and soon, she was stepping off onto the towpath with the mid line and taking a turn round the wooden bollard. When the boat had stopped moving, she tied a knot called a clove hitch in the mid line and dropped it over the bollard, keeping the boat tight in to the bank. Then she walked up the steps beside the lock with the windlass in her hand. This was a metal handle that was used to wind up the paddles on the lock gates in order to empty or fill the lock. The lock was already empty as a boat had recently passed through it going downhill.

Trip Boat Tim was sitting on a seat outside his cottage with a coil of thick rope on his lap. He was pushing a wooden tool through the rope so he could open it up and push another strand through. He was making a back splice, which would stop the end of the rope from coming apart. Tim had been born in the cottage in 1948 and had lived there all his life. His father had been the lockkeeper here and had looked after five miles of the canal and all of the locks on it. When Tim's dad retired, his part of the canal was joined with another and looked after by someone else. Tim bought the cottage from British Waterways after his dad died. He had learned a lot of skills from his father over the years and had become a good mechanic and engineer. Many of the local boaters were very happy to pay him to do repairs to their boats.

Tim's dog Barney was lying at his feet. "Don't think he's too well," said Tim, "didn't eat any dinner yesterday."

Peggy bent down to stroke Barney.

"They have their off days, just like us."

Tim had got Barney from a Border Collie rescue centre in North Wales. He had only been a year old but had instantly taken to life on the canals. Tim's previous dog, Paddy, a black Labrador, had died at 14. He had been a wonderful dog and companion but would want to spend more time in the water than on the boat or the bank.

Peggy pushed on the heavy balance beam opening the gate into the lock. As she steered the boat in, there was a long iron ladder that reached to the top of the lock. When the boat drew level, Peggy took the engine out of gear and put it into neutral. Then, taking the mid line, she climbed up the ladder to the top of the lock with her windlass tucked into her leather belt. Peggy pulled the boat into the side of the lock chamber and secured it to a bollard, then closed the gate behind her. As she did so, Tim had already put his windlass onto the ground paddles of the gate in front of the boat. "OK, Tim," she said, "paddles up."

The water in the chamber started to bubble and churn as the lock began to fill. When it was high enough, Tim put the windlass on the gate paddles and wound those up, too. A great gush of water poured into the lock from the canal above, lifting the boat upwards. When the water level was the same as the canal, Tim was able to push open the gate. Peggy undid the line, stepped onto the stern of the boat and steered out of the lock.

"I'm going to moor outside the shop."

"See you later," called Tim, closing the gate behind her.

Peggy stopped outside the canal shop, turned off the engine and went inside to see Jean. The red brick building that housed the canal shop was over 200 years old and had once been the toll house, where load -carrying boats would have to pay to go through the lock. Now it sold souvenirs of the waterways; postcards, books, and of course, Peggy's canal art, painted in wonderful reds, greens and yellows. There was a small section for sweets, groceries and drinks and a whole wall covered in maps and pictures of the waterways. Peggy loved the ones taken in the winter, when the canal was iced over and all the surrounding fields white with snow. For sale in the corner of the shop were two bow fenders for the front of boats and one button fender for the back end. Tim had made all of these from long lengths of rope. They took a long time to make and he would wait until the winter months when the camper boats were not being used and the dark came early. There was a wooden box with an assortment of short - and long-handled windlasses for opening the locks, mooring spikes and some long canes with fishing nets at the end. Outside in a large plastic bin were footballs, cricket sets, Frisbees and swing balls – and a red wooden bench where Wills, Jean's large, black tom cat, would spend the day sleeping in the sun. At night, he would hunt wood mice, leaving them on the doorstep for Jean to find in the morning. In the back garden, she kept some Rhode Island Red hens and sold the freshly laid eggs in the shop, along with her well known homemade fruit jams and cakes. Then there was Jack, the big white goose who was better at guarding the canal shop and garden than any noisy dog. Jean had to make sure the gate was closed or he would chase people down the towpath. He particularly disliked cyclists and would try to peck their ankles as they rode by.

On the other side of the canal opposite the shop were the former stables. Nowadays, they were used by British Waterways to store equipment for repairing the locks. This is where the horses that used to pull the boats along the canal, in the days before they had engines, used to rest overnight. Now, a small blue tug and a crane mounted on a flat barge were moored in front of the building. They would carry the heavy equipment and new lock gates along the canal to be fitted by the workmen.

Jean had got together all of the provisions that Peggy had asked her for. She pointed to a cardboard box on the counter. There were some eggs and freshly baked bread, milk and sausages from Oak Farm and a pot of Jean's homemade strawberry jam.

"Will that be enough food?"

Peggy laughed. "I should hope so" she said, "There is only me to feed."

She carried the box to the boat, followed by Wills the tom cat. The stern hatch was partly open. Peggy thought it odd, as she was sure it had been closed when she had left the boat. Climbing down the steps, she walked through the back cabin and past the heads, where the toilet and shower were. She unpacked the groceries and put them onto the shelves in the galley. Wills followed.

"You coming as well are you?" she laughed.

Jean called her from the stern of the boat. "Peggy – you forgot the butter!"

Peggy climbed back up the steps.

"Thanks, Jean. I'd better get under way. See you on Wednesday."

"Have a good trip," said her friend.

She picked up a grumpy Wills and walked back to the canal shop. Peggy turned the ignition key and untied the lines before pushing off the stern. She was on her way.

Peggy knew a lot of the boat people on the canal. As she passed their moored boats, some would wave or call out. They all remembered the fire on Turtle and were happy to see Peggy steering a boat on the canal once again. Most lived on board narrow boats, but some lived on houseboats. These were bigger than narrow boats and didn't have an engine, but stayed tied up to the moorings all the time. Some had a small dinghy with an outboard motor or a canoe tied up alongside. The owners had built little gardens on the bank. Some had lots of flowers with small lawns while others had vegetable plots with wooden sheds where they kept their tools and gardening equipment. When Peggy reached the end of the line of moored boats, she pushed the throttle down to speed up. Moored boaters did get upset if passing boats went by too fast, as the wash made their boat rock and bang against the side of the bank. There were no more locks until after she had passed through the swing bridge, so Peggy sat on the stern rail with the warm breeze blowing through her hair.

At 60 feet, Kingfisher was a bigger boat than Turtle had been, and had a cruiser stern, which meant that you had more space to move about on the back deck and the engine was outside the cabin and underneath the stern boards. Turtle had been a traditional-style stern which had a smaller space to stand when steering but more room inside the boat, and the engine was inside as well, which Peggy liked. As she passed under a low willow tree, an electric blue male dragonfly darted to and fro just above the surface of the water before disappearing into the reflection of the sun.

Up ahead, a group of fishermen had their fishing poles across the canal; they were so long they almost reached to the opposite bank. As Peggy went by, they lifted them up like a drawbridge so she could pass underneath.

"Any luck?" Peggy called to one of the fishermen, who was sitting outside his little green tent that was pitched on the side of the towpath. He lifted his keep net out of the water to show Peggy his catch. "Not bad," he replied, "couple of bream and a perch."

In the distance, two hot air balloons floated silently across the sky. One of them was shaped like a huge blue flame and the other was bright orange. Peggy watched them until they disappeared behind a low white fluffy cloud. She loved this stretch of the canal. A carpet of yellow water lilies, which she knew as "brandy bottle" because of their flask shaped fruits, grew at the margins of the canal, sending a faint scent of stale alcohol into the air. The hedgerow was a green corridor bursting with wild fruit and flowers and alive with insects and birds. Often, when she had her own narrow boat, she would come here for a weekend, and particularly liked it in the spring, when a blanket of bluebells covered the floor of the nearby woods.

She rounded the bend by the stables, where the railway line crossed the canal. A fast intercity train from Paddington to Bristol thundered by, disturbing some pigeons that were resting on the beams underneath the bridge. By the time Peggy had come out the other side, it had disappeared into the distance. Peggy hated speed and big cities. She was a country girl at heart and preferred the slow pace of the canals.

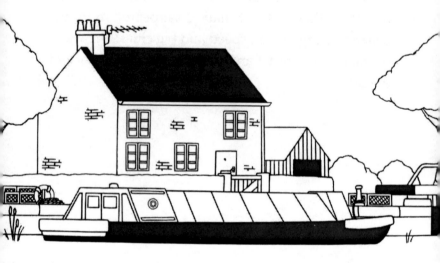

CHAPTER TWO:

Zed - The Stowaway

The swing bridge crossed the canal, so that the farmer could move his cattle from one field to another. The bridge was too low for boats to pass beneath so boaters wanting to go through would have to moor up their boat and then open and close the bridge before continuing. The bridge was painted white with railings on each side and had a big padlock and chain that had to be opened with a special British Waterways key. Peggy moored Kingfisher by the swing bridge and went down into the galley to make a cup of tea. She had just put the kettle on when she heard a bump come from inside the front cabin.

She wondered if Wills had crept back onto the boat before she had set off. She pushed open the cabin door. There was a double bed with a blue duvet, a small sink with a round mirror and two tall wooden doors, which was the front of the wardrobe. Just as Peggy thought she must have been imagining it, a sound came from inside the wardrobe. It was a scraping noise as if someone had moved the metal coat hangers along the rail. Quickly, she pulled opened the wardrobe door.

"Good grief," she said with a start.

Sitting on the floor of the wardrobe was the small, grubby, red-haired boy from the circus. "What on earth are you doing here in this wardrobe, on this boat?" Peggy asked.

The small boy looked up.

"Please, lady – don't send me back. Don't tell. I've run away from the circus."

"Run away? I thought people ran away to the circus, not away from it!" she exclaimed.

She bent down and took the boy's arm.

"Right, come on, young fella, up you come."

Tears were now starting to run down his grimy cheeks.

"I 'ate it there, and I 'ate 'im!"

"Who?" asked Peggy.

"Uncle Darren."

"Is that the man I saw shouting at you?"

"Yer," he sobbed, "'e always shouts at me, 'e makes me work for nuffink and I never get no dinner!"

"Well, this is a real problem, isn't it? Do you have a name, boy?"

"Zed 'Awkins," he replied.

"Zed – that's a nice name. My name is Peggy. How old are you, Zed?"

"I'm 11, nearly 12."

Peggy was shocked. How could someone make an 11-year-old work like that? He should be in school!

"So it was you that opened the hatch at the stern of the boat," she said.

Zed nodded. "Yeah sorry, missus. It was when you stopped at the shop. I was 'iding behind the tree."

Peggy thought how thin he looked.

"When did you last eat something, Zed?"

"Last night. I nicked an 'otdog from the stall at the circus."

"When did you last have a shower?"

"Never 'ad one. I've 'ad a bath before, though."

Peggy laughed. "Well that's something."

She sat on the bed next to him.

"Right, Zed – this is what we're going to do. I'm going to show you how to work the shower, and then

we're going to have something nice to eat, and then....
Well, let's worry about that after, shall we?"

Zed spent ages in the shower. "Come on, Zed,"
called Peggy, "we'll run out of water." She would
have to fill the boat's water tank again if he took
much longer!

She handed him a large, clean, pink bath towel
that she had in her bag.

"Once you've dried yourself, I want you to wrap
up warm in the duvet on the bed and I'll bring you
something hot to eat," she said. "Don't put those
dirty old clothes back on."

After Zed had eaten a plate of sausages and beans
with some thick crusty bread and jam, he fell fast
asleep on the bed. Peggy picked up his dirty clothes
and threw them in a black bin bag. She sat on the bed
beside him.

"Well, Peggy, old girl," she said to herself, "now
what do we do?"

She called Trip Boat Tim on her mobile.

"I've got a problem."

"What sort of problem?" Tim asked.

"Well, it's 11 years old, goes by the name of Zed,
and comes from the circus. I've found him on the
boat."

Tim thought for a moment.

"We're not talking about that young lad who was
selling programmes, are we?"

"Indeed we are."

"Well, I never!" said Tim. "The cheeky little so-and-so!" He was just about to ask more questions, but Peggy stopped him.

"I'll tell you about it later. The point is, now what do I do? I've already thrown his clothes away – they were filthy."

"So what's he wearing?" asked Tim.

"The duvet," said Peggy.

Tim needed time to think.

"Keep the phone close by," he said, "I'll ring you back."

Peggy went back into the front cabin. Zed was still fast asleep. "How could people treat children like this?" she thought to herself. "Poor little mite. He just doesn't deserve it."

Tim rang back about half an hour later.

"I phoned Janice Phillips at the village school. I'm collecting her at home and driving over to you. She's bringing some clothes that belong to her son. Sit tight and we'll be with you in about an hour." "OK," said Peggy. "See you soon. I'll have the kettle on."

Tim and Mrs. Phillips arrived in his old brown Land Rover with the open back that was always full up with tools and parts of narrow boat engines. He drove it along the dirt track and parked alongside the swing bridge. Barney jumped from the back. Zed had woken up and was sitting with Peggy in the saloon cabin, drinking hot chocolate and eating ginger biscuits. She had told him they were coming and that

22

he was to trust them.

"Knock, knock," shouted Tim, before pushing open the front doors.

"This is Tim and Mrs. Phillips," Peggy said to Zed, "The people I was telling you about."

"Hello," said Tim, holding out his large hand for Zed to shake.

Tim looked a little unusual. He was a tall man with a brown, weather-beaten face, a thick droopy moustache and a short, stubbly beard. He wore an old, patched woollen jumper, a red scarf around his neck, and trousers held up by a thick leather belt. He also had strong leather boots with metal toe caps, to protect his toes when he was working with heavy engines. On his head, he wore an old, oil-stained hat. Barney, his dog, also had a thin red scarf around his neck.

Janice Phillips sat on the small sofa next to Zed. She had a kind face, and Zed soon felt at ease with her. She was young to be a head teacher, although the village school was very small, with only six classes. She had long brown hair and tinted glasses with pink frames, and wore a long, cool blue dress with white shoes. In the mornings, she could often be seen running along the towpath and last year, she had competed in the London Marathon. "I have some clean clothes for you, Zed," she said. "They belong to my son, Luke. I hope they're OK – you look about the same size. Why don't you pop into the cabin and get dressed, and then we can talk."

Zed looked at Peggy.

"Go on, love."

Zed went to change.

"So what do we do now?" asked Peggy.

"We need to find out a bit more about him and see if he has any other family," said Janice, "Then, of course, we have to tell the police, in case they're looking for him."

"I very much doubt that," Peggy said, and told Janice and Tim about the uncle.

Zed came back into the saloon cabin, dressed in his new clothes.

"Well, well," laughed Peggy, "it's a new boy."

"Ain't never 'ad good gear like this," he said, sitting down next to Peggy.

"Zed," said Janice, "I am the head teacher at St. Mark's – the local junior school in the village. Did you go to school?"

"Used to, when I lived with me Gran."

"Where was that?"

"London."

"Did you like living there?"

"It was alright."

"What about your Mum and Dad?"

"Never knew me Dad, and Mum 'ad to go away last year."

"What do you mean, 'away'?" Tim asked.

"Just away – that's why Gran thought I should go

with me Uncle Darren to the circus."

Seeing that Zed was getting a bit upset, Peggy interrupted. "Tim, how about you take Zed outside for a while?"

"Hey, Zed – I've got my fishing rod in the Land Rover," Tim said. "Have you ever fished before?"

"No, never."

"Come on, then. Let's see if we can catch a fish."

Zed smiled and followed Tim outside to the old Land Rover. From the back, Tim took a long brown leather bag with pockets in the side, and then handed Zed two folding metal chairs. "Put them up on the bank," he said, "just over there by the bridge."

They both sat on the chairs while Tim unzipped the bag. He pulled out three separate sections of fishing rod and pushed them all together to make one long bendy rod. He showed Zed how to put the reel onto the rod and then pulled a long length of line through the little metal hoops that ran along it. On the end of the line, he tied a sharp looking hook with a blood knot and attached a float and some weights about twelve inches above the hook.

"Right," said Tim, "would you like to put the maggot on?"

He took the top off of a round plastic container full of wriggling maggots. "Take one out."

Zed slowly put his hand in and lifted out one maggot. Tim held out the hook.

"Push it carefully over the sharp bit, that's called

the barb, and mind your finger."

"Ah! It's burst!" shouted Zed.

"So would you if someone stuck a big hook in you!"

Zed laughed.

Tim returned to the Land Rover and brought back a landing net and a keep net. He put the keep net into the water and secured it to the bank.

"If we catch a big fish, I want you to use the landing net, Zed. As I pull it into the bank, you put the landing net underneath it. That way, we don't tear the fish's mouth when we pull it out."

Tim stood up, and holding the rod over his shoulder, brought it forward with a loud swish. The line uncoiled, sending the hook and float flying into the middle of the canal. After reeling the line back in, he passed the rod to Zed. He showed him how to hold it and work the reel. Zed did exactly what Tim had said.

"Well done Zed, that's a good cast. Are you sure you haven't done this before?"

"No – 'onest, Tim."

"Right – sit down and place the rod on the stand."

"Will we catch any fish?"

"Well, that depends on how quiet we are and how hard we concentrate on the float. As soon as it's pulled down under the water, it means a fish has taken the bait, and that's when we strike."

They sat next to each other in the warm evening

sun: Tim, the reluctant bachelor, who had always wanted a son to show how to fish and handle boats, and Zed, a boy of 11 who had never known his father and had spent most of his life on a South London housing estate or working in a circus.

"What can you hear, Zed?"

Zed thought for a moment.

"Nuffink."

"Exactly. Isn't it wonderful?"

"It's gone, quick!" shouted Zed, pointing to the float.

Tim lifted the rod with a jerk and started to reel in the line.

"Is there a fish?"

"I think so, but don't get too excited – it may be an old bike," laughed Tim, as the rod started to bend. "Grab the landing net, Zed, and hold it in the water."

Just then, a loud splash broke the surface.

"I saw it!" shouted Zed. "It's a fish, its huge!"

"Slowly does it." Tim pulled the fish closer to the bank. Zed was now standing on the edge of the bank with the landing net.

"Be careful – we don't want you joining the fish in the canal."

Tim asked Zed to put the landing net underneath the fish and bring it onto the bank. Zed placed it carefully on the ground. Tim took an old piece of rag from his pocket and carefully lifted the fish out of the net.

"Now we have to get the hook out."

"What sort of fish is it?"

"It's a carp – you can tell by the small bronze-coloured scales all over it."

"Can I touch it?" asked Zed.

"You shouldn't touch it with your bare hands. Because our skin is warm, you can burn its flesh. But if you take the rag and hold it still, I'll get the hook out."

"Its 'eavy," said Zed.

"Yes, it's a good size. I reckon it weighs about four pounds."

Tim quickly removed the hook and Zed dropped it into the keep net with a splash. They were just about to put some more bait on the hook when Peggy appeared from inside the boat. Zed called Peggy over.

"Come and see this fish we've got, it's big!"

He lifted up the keep net to show Peggy their prize.

"Well done – what a catch!"

"Can we catch another one?" asked Zed.

"I think we need to go aboard the boat and sort out what's going to happen to you, young man," said Peggy. "She's right," agreed Tim. "Are you going to let our fish go, then?"

Zed knelt on the bank and lifted the keep net out of the water. "Bye, bye, fish."

On board Kingfisher, they sat around a small

wooden table in the saloon cabin. Outside, it was getting dark.

"Zed," said Janice Phillips, "you mentioned your grandmother. Do you have a phone number for her?"

"No," said Zed, "but I know where she lives."

"What we don't understand is why your Gran let your uncle take you away to the circus – or what happened to your mother."

He was quiet for a moment. "She's in prison in London, and I'd got chucked out of school, so Gran thought I should live with me uncle when 'e went back to the circus."

Tim shook his head. Zed looked at him.

"She don't know what 'e's like."

Janice Phillips told Zed that while he was fishing with Tim, she had spoken to Constable Thomas, the village policeman and also to a friend of hers at Social Services. Zed moved closer to Peggy.

"I 'aven't got to go back to the circus, 'ave I?"

"No you haven't, love, but we need to get in contact with your Gran – that would be the best thing to do. Are you happy with that?"

"Will she get into trouble for letting me go with me uncle?"

"I hope not," said Janice. "I am sure she thought she was doing the right thing, but we do need to contact her and let her know what's going on. Do you know the address, Zed?"

He did. It was Nelson Block, number 35, Heather

29

Road, Rotherhithe, in South London.

"What about a phone number, love?" Peggy asked.

"No, not any more. I used to be able to ring Gran on me uncle's mobile, but 'e said it cost too much."

It was late and getting very dark outside. Tim had suggested that he stayed with Peggy and Zed, and Janice took his Land Rover back to the village. They had lost a lot of time being moored at the swing bridge and still had to get the boat to Boswell's Yard by Wednesday evening, otherwise Kingfisher would lose its slot in the dry dock. Janice said she would sort out getting in contact with Zed's Gran and let PC Thomas know what was happening. She took Tim's Land Rover keys and the bag with Zed's old, dirty clothes.

"I'll get rid of these," she said. "I'll ring you tomorrow."

Tim walked her to the Land Rover and took his fishing gear out of the back.

"Drive carefully," he shouted as she pulled away. He wasn't sure if she had ever driven a Land Rover before, let alone an old one like his without any power steering.

"Well, young Zed," said Peggy, "I think it's time you were in bed."

"Can I 'ave another shower?"

"I think you're clean enough," laughed Peggy.

"Goodnight, Zed," called Tim as he disappeared into the front cabin.

"Night, Tim – fanks for taking me fishing!"

Zed fell asleep as soon as his head hit the pillow.

Peggy and Tim sat outside on the bow seats, drinking from two large mugs of hot chocolate. Midges clustered around the light from the small hurricane lamp that Tim had lit and stood on the roof of the boat.

"I'll come with you tomorrow, but we need to get an early start if we're going to get the boat to Boswell's by Wednesday evening," said Tim. "Thanks. We'll have an extra crew member now," said Peggy. "What worries me is what happens to him after we get to Boswell's Yard."

"It's a real shame," said Tim.

They sat in silence for a long time alone with their thoughts and dreams. Tim finished his drink and went to bed. Peggy stayed up a little longer, watching the bats swoop low over the canal before climbing back into their dark world. It was good to have Tim on board, and Zed, too – although he hadn't been an invited guest. It gave her someone to look after. "Even a 60-year-old can dream of what might have been," she thought.

The following morning, Janice Philips rang the school to say she would be in late. She went to the police house in the village to meet Constable Thomas. She asked him to visit the circus and speak to Zed's Uncle Darren. Constable Thomas arrived just after eleven o'clock in the morning. The circus was moving on. The big top tent lay in a heap of rumpled canvas on the grass, while a gang of strong men were using sledgehammers to loosen the large metal stakes that had held the guy lines in place. Constable Thomas recognised two of them as the trapeze artists. He, too, had visited the circus with his wife and two children.

The brightly coloured caravans and trailers had been hitched onto vans and lorries, ready to leave the field. The entrance archway and sign were being lowered slowly to the ground and the horses were being led up a ramp into a horse box. Soon, all that would be left from the circus would be the well-trodden grass and dusty wheel tracks of the vehicles.

There was no sign of Zed's Uncle Darren. A long vehicle loaded with dodgem cars was reversing near to where they stood. PC Thomas walked over to speak to the driver.

"Morning," he said, "I'm looking for Darren."

"There's a surprise," replied the driver.

"Do you know where I might find him?"

"Go behind that white lorry with the metal poles on. There's an old grey caravan, he'll be in there."

"Thanks mate."

He walked to the caravan and gave a loud bang on the door. After a few minutes, Darren opened the door. He didn't look happy to see a police uniform. PC Thomas explained that they wanted to talk to him about Zed Hawkins.

Darren sighed. "You'd better come in, I suppose."

As they entered the caravan, there was a smell of fried food in the air. There were two long cushioned bench seats – one piled high with unwashed clothes. In the sink were a stack of plates and pots and a greasy frying pan sat on the small two-ring stove. PC Thomas assumed the benches doubled as beds and that this was where Zed had slept.

"Can I ask your relationship to Zed Hawkins?" asked PC Thomas.

"Yeah," said Darren. "I'm his uncle."

His long, black, greasy hair touched the dirty collar of his blue shirt. His teeth were a yellow colour and his fingers stained with nicotine from too much smoking. PC Thomas took a step back to avoid Darren's breath, which stank of alcohol.

"'Is mother, Amanda, she's my sister. So what's 'e been up to?"

"Do you know where he is?" asked PC Thomas.

"No, 'e cleared off the other night."

"What do you mean cleared off? He's only 11, and you didn't even report him missing?"

Darren shrugged. "He ain't my problem. I only said I'd take 'im 'cos 'is mother's in the nick and 'e'd been chucked out of school."

"Do you know why she was sent to prison?" asked PC Thomas.

"Nicking stuff from a shop, then she clouted one of your lot when she was being arrested."

"Could I take your full name, sir?"

"'Awkins. Darren 'Awkins."

""I understand, Mr. Hawkins, that Zed lived with his grandmother in South London?"

"Yeah, that's right – she's me mother."

"Do you have a phone number for her?"

Darren went to the pocket of his jacket and pulled out a mobile. Scrolling down, he called out a number for Zed's Gran, which PC Thomas wrote down in his notebook.

"I would like your mobile number as well and the location of your next stop with the circus."

PC Thomas put his notebook into his back pocket. "Right, sir, I have to inform you that we have Zed in safe care and we will be contacting his grandmother, who I understand has custody of him whilst his mother is in prison. We may need to talk to you again, as well. This is a serious business." Darren shrugged again.

"Suit yerself, mate."

CHAPTER THREE:

Zed's First Boat Trip

Tim had woken early on Tuesday morning, as he always did. Barney, who had slept the night on Zed's bed, was eating porridge from a plastic bowl on the floor.

"Morning, Tim." Peggy stumbled half asleep into the saloon. "What time is it?"

"It's seven o'clock."

"I need a coffee, a strong one," she said, falling into a chair.

Peggy showered, and then woke Zed. Tim had already checked the engine for oil and water and was eager to get going. While Zed washed, Peggy fried some eggs and bacon and cut thick slices of brown bread.

"Right, Zed," said Tim, "it's time to earn your keep, young man." He passed Zed a buoyancy aid and showed him how to put it on and do up the buckle at the front.

"Now – all the time that you're outside on the boat, you keep that on. Got it?"

Zed nodded. "OK, Tim."

"Good. Let's go, crew. Action stations!"

Peggy and Zed followed Tim onto the towpath. Tim asked Peggy to go ahead and open the swing bridge. He wanted to explain the parts of the boat to Zed before they set off.

"So is this the first time you've been on a boat, Zed?" asked Tim. Zed nodded.

They climbed up a grassy bank so they were looking down onto the boat.

"Right, let's start with the parts of the boat you need to know." He pointed to the front.

"That's the sharp end. It's called the bow. The back, the blunt end is called the stern. The two ropes you can see on each end are called the bowline and stern line."

"What's that big pole on the roof for?" asked Zed.

"It's called a barge pole. If we run aground, we can push ourselves off with that, and the plank next to it, that's called a brow. You may have heard it called a gangplank."

"What, like the pirates used to make people walk along?"

"You got it, Zed."

"Do you get pirates on the canal, Tim?"

"Well I've never come across any, not yet, but you never know! Let's go and stand on the stern of the boat, Zed."

As Zed stood, Barney jumped up, sending him rolling down the grass bank onto the towpath below. Tim watched as Zed lay on the grass laughing while Barney licked his face. Standing on the cruiser stern, he explained to Zed that the right hand side of the boat was called the starboard and the left side was called port.

Peggy had pushed open the swing bridge and was waving for them to go through. Tim left Zed with his hand on the tiller while he untied the bowline and stern line. He gave the boat a push sideways and jumped on. Standing next to Zed, he steered the boat through the gap and came alongside the bank on the other side of the bridge. All the time, Zed had kept his hand on the tiller, watching everything that Tim did. Peggy closed the bridge and jumped on board.

"Let's go," said Tim, pushing the throttle forward.

The morning mist had cleared and the sun was coming through. It was going to be a warm day. There was a supermarket alongside the canal in the next town and Peggy needed to get some more food. She had only brought enough for one and now there were three of them to feed – four, including Barney. They passed a recently built golf course, which used to be farmland. Tim told Zed how one day the farmer had accidentally shot and killed his son while out hunting for rabbits. He was so full of remorse that a week later he shot himself with the same gun. Soon afterwards, the farm was sold. "They say that his ghost has been seen on the golf course near to the spot where he shot his son," said Tim. "What, a real ghost?" asked Zed.

"Oh yes, it's real, alright."

"'Ave you seen ghosts on the canal, Tim?"

"Many times, and if you sit quietly on a lock gate just as the sun is going down, you may see them, too."

Zed was sitting on the roof facing Tim listening carefully to every word.

"You have to look into the shadows – that's where they are – and if you are very still you may hear them, also."

"What, do they talk?"

"It's like a low whisper on the breeze, and sometimes you can hear the panting of the horses as they pulled the boats along the towpath into the lock.

But as I say, you have to be very still."

Peggy pushed Zed's gangly legs aside as she came up the back steps onto the stern.

"Peggy, did you know there are ghosts on the canal and you can 'ear 'em talking?"

She smiled at Tim. "So I've heard love, so I've heard."

They went under a bridge where a busy main road passed overhead and then around a very sharp left hand bend and into a wide part of the canal. Tim explained to Zed that this was called a "winding hole" and it was where boats could turn around. There was another sharp bend to the right, with a brick bridge, painted white. Tim pushed hard on the tiller bar and gave the throttle a little burst of speed. Kingfisher glided through the narrow bridge hole without even touching the sides.

"Tim's showing off," Peggy said to Zed.

"No I'm not! It's skill, pure skill."

Zed laughed and took off his buoyancy aid and T-shirt to sunbathe on the roof.

"You're forgetting something, young man" called Tim, "put the buoyancy aid back on."

The canal twisted its way between green fields and hedgerows, occasionally running alongside or under a road. Zed slept. Barney slept. Peggy dozed at the bow under her straw hat. Tim sat on the stern rail, his hand resting lightly on the tiller bar. His thoughts were concentrated on a sparrow hawk that was high in the sky and preparing to swoop on its next meal.

As they entered the outskirts of the town, a new housing estate was being built on both sides of the canal. Soon, there would be "no mooring" signs put up and fewer places for boaters to stop in the future, thought Tim. They passed the back of an industrial estate, where there was a huge plastic model of a spaceman sitting astride a rocket. Zed asked Tim if he thought they needed it and if not, whether they could take it and put in on the roof of the boat. Tim gently explained that it wouldn't be very practical, particularly when passing under low bridges. Sitting on the opposite side of the canal were a group of scruffy men drinking from cans of beer and bottles of wine. They waved and shouted something which Tim didn't understand.

"Who are they?" asked Zed.

Tim said they were the local drunks and were always there.

"Like me uncle – 'e was always drunk," said Zed.

Ahead was the bridge that carried the high street over the canal and then beyond was the new supermarket where they would moor so Peggy could stock up on provisions. She had also decided to buy Zed some more clothes.

"Ready with the bowline," called Tim.

Peggy waited until the bow ran alongside the bank, and then stepped out with the line. Zed did the same with the stern line. When the boat had come to a stop, Tim and Peggy passed the lines through the mooring rings and tied them off around the cleats on the boat. Barney jumped off and cocked his leg up the nearest bush.

While Peggy and Zed went shopping, Tim and Barney decided to crash out on the bed in the stern cabin. After buying the food, including some chocolate ice cream for Zed, they walked through to the clothes section. Although Mrs Phillips had brought some of her son's clothes for Zed, Peggy felt he should have some of his own. He picked out some T-shirts, a pair of jeans, some shorts, underwear, a pair of trainers and a small rucksack. Peggy later told Tim that Zed's face was a picture of happiness that she would always remember. She didn't tell him that Zed had also given her a big hug. She thought that he would find that silly. Tim was not given to signs of emotion, at least not outwardly, and Peggy often thought he had more feelings for boats and dogs than people. That's not to say he wasn't a kind person – but he was very cautious.

When they arrived back on the boat, Tim and Barney were fast asleep on the bed. Zed couldn't wait to put his new clothes on, particularly the trainers; he had worn a pair before, but never like these.

"Wow" said Peggy, "look at you, very trendy."

Zed told Peggy that he had never had new clothes before and always got hand-me-downs from Conner.

"Who is Conner?"

"'E's my stepbrother. 'E lives with 'is Dad, though."

"How old is he?"

"Firteen, but he's a bit fick."

"What do you mean, a bit thick?"

"Well, 'e can't read or write."

"So he's got learning difficulties?"

"Yer, summink like that, 'e gets in a right strop."

A loud yawn came from the back cabin.

"Shove the kettle on, somebody."

"Yes, sir," shouted Peggy. "Your wish is our command."

Zed ran to the back of the boat to show Tim his new clothes.

"Blimey!" said Tim, "a new man! I could do with a T-shirt like that."

"You wouldn't wear it unless it had engine oil on," shouted Peggy, as she prepared a lunch of French bread with cheese and pickle followed by chocolate ice cream.

After lunch, Tim sat at the bow reading his newspaper while Peggy and Zed took Barney for a walk along the towpath.

"Peggy," Zed asked, "Do you and Tim 'ave any kids?"

Peggy laughed. "How do you mean, me and Tim?"

"Well, most married people 'ave kids."

"Good Lord, Zed, Tim and me aren't married,

love, we're just very good friends."

"You could still 'ave kids."

Peggy felt her cheeks starting to flush. "I don't think so love, I don't think so."

"I wish I 'ad someone like you and Tim as my mum and dad," he said before running up a grassy bank after Barney. Peggy felt a lump come into her throat.

Back at the boat, Tim was sitting on the stern with the engine running. "Come on you two, let's go! Grab the bowline, Zed, I'll do the stern."

Kingfisher moved gently away from the bank and they headed towards the aqueduct, which was about a mile away.

"What's an aqueduct?" asked Zed, as they neared the narrow steel channel.

Tim explained that it was a bridge for carrying a canal or river over a valley, or a road, or a river.

"Hope you have a head for heights. We're a long way up."

Zed was taking no chances and moved off the roof where he had been sitting and stood next to Tim. "What's that river down there, Tim?"

"That's the Avon. It runs alongside the canal for some way."

"Bet there's some good fish in there."

"Yes, there is. Shame we haven't got time to stop."

After the aqueduct, there was a sharp right hand turn past a rubbish disposal and a fresh water point.

Tim slowed down as a group of youngsters rafted up together in brightly coloured kayaks started to break away from each other. They weren't much older than Zed and were in the charge of two instructors. It was only when Tim got nearer that he recognised Dean Cherry from the outdoor activity centre.

"Afternoon, Dean," he called.

Dean paddled over and held onto the side of the narrow boat. He was about 25 and was wearing a red helmet and a blue buoyancy aid. Covering the cockpit was a spray deck to stop the water from going into the kayak.

"Hi guys. Who's this young man, then?"

"It's a long story, Dean. He's our little stowaway. His name is Zed."

Dean held out his wet hand for Zed to shake.

"Hey, that's cool, man – a real live stowaway! Good to meet you, Zed. Have you ever been in a kayak before?"

"No, never."

Tim shook his head. "Sorry, mate, we just haven't got the time."

"That's a shame, but I'm sure we'll meet again, Zed."

Just then, there was a loud splash and lots of laughter from the other youngsters. One of them had capsized and was swimming in the canal next to his kayak.

"Better go, guys," said Dean, and with a flick of

44

his paddle, he spun around and headed towards the swimming youngster. Tim pushed the throttle forward and Kingfisher moved slowly past them.

"Bring him to the activity centre one day," shouted Dean.

Tim nodded and waved. Dean didn't know that after tomorrow, Tim and Peggy might never see Zed again.

"Have you been in a kayak before, Tim?" asked Zed.

He laughed. "Only once, and I came straight out the other side. I don't think I'm built for kayaks. I'm too top heavy."

After leaving the group at the end of the aqueduct, they made good time. Tim was surprised how few boats were on the canal, particularly at this time of year. At the height of the season, it was possible to wait for an hour to get through a lock. There weren't many locks on this stretch and those they did have to go through were all in their favour, which meant they didn't have to empty them first. After Peggy had showed him how to work his first lock, Zed had quickly mastered how to use a windlass and helped Peggy push open the heavy gates and handle the lines. He was also getting a little too confident and got a mild telling off from Tim when he jumped from the bank onto the gunwales before the boat was alongside.

"You'll make a lovely soft fender, Zed," said Tim.

"What's a fender?"

"It's something that goes between the boat and the bank to stop damage to the side, and you were nearly it," replied Tim.

Peggy decided to walk to the next lock with Barney. She pretended that it was him who needed the exercise. He didn't seem impressed and tried to jump on the boat as it came out of the lock, but it was too far out from the side.

"Right, young Zed," said Tim, "I need a cup of tea. Do you reckon that you can keep this great vessel in a straight line?"

"What, on me own?"

"Indeed, just you. I'm off to put the kettle on."

"I could make the tea," said Zed, worried about being left on his own.

"No, thanks. I remember the cup you made earlier. It was like dishwater."

Tim disappeared down below. Zed stood proudly with his hand resting on the polished brass tiller bar. In front was sixty foot of shining blue narrow boat, and he was in charge – he was the skipper. If only Mum and Gran could see me now, he thought.

Tim deliberately stayed down below, looking out from the front door until they came to a sharp bend just before the next lock. Peggy was already there and had opened the gates so that they could go straight in. Zed kept his hand on the tiller while Tim steered it in. Peggy took the bowline.

"Well done," said Tim, "a good bit of steering. We'll make a boatman out of you yet, Zed." They moored up on the other side of the lock so Tim could remove an object that had tangled itself around the propeller.

"It's probably a plastic bag or some old rope," he told Zed.

After stopping the engine, he removed the ignition keys and then showed Zed how to take the top of the weed hatch off. He put his hand into the water until he could feel the propeller.

"Pass me the knife, please, Zed."

Zed watched as Tim cut two thick pieces of nylon rope from the propeller. He passed them to Zed, who put them on the roof. He explained to Zed the importance of putting the hatch back securely; otherwise water could come in and could sink the boat.

Nobody said much for the next few miles. Tim steered the boat. Peggy was busy in the galley making some ship's biscuits. She always cooked when she wanted to lose herself and Zed sat on the bow with Barney just watching as the landscape unfolded. It reminded him of a pop-up picture book he had as a child, where each page would show a different scene. Horses lazing in a farm field with red and white wooden fences and jumps. The marina, hidden beyond the small bridge hole, filled with an assortment of different coloured narrow boats and little cruisers. The flight of locks stretching down to the bottom of the hill reminded Zed of a line of dominoes, where if you pushed one, they would all fall over. He saw the outstretched silver grey wings of a heron against the background of a green hedgerow and the little black and white moorhens busily building a floating nest at the canal edge.

"Pirates!" shouted Zed pointing ahead, and indeed there were.

A narrow boat flying the skull and crossbones flag was coming towards them. Standing on the bow of the boat was a young man with a pirate's hat, a plastic sword, and a long black coat with gold rings on the sleeves. The rest of the all male crew were also dressed as pirates. One was standing on the roof with no shirt, a scarf tied round his head, a large earring and red dye smeared on his bare chest.

"Ahoy, shipmates, prepare to be boarded," he called waving a plastic pistol. Their boat was getting closer. Tim recognised straight away that they were just out having a party and were slightly drunk. But for Zed, they looked just like the real pirates he'd seen in that film on telly.

"Ooh, arrr," shouted the captain. What be your name, boy?"

"I'm Zed."

"Are you the cabin boy, Zed?"

Before he had time to reply Peggy came out of the front door. "No, he's a stowaway."

"Shiver me timbers, then he needs to walk the plank."

Another pirate with a stuffed green parrot clipped to his shoulder and a black eye patch had jumped onto the bow of Kingfisher.

"Right me hearties, have ye any treasure on board?"

"What about some freshly made ship's biscuits?" called Peggy.

"Ooh arrr, that will do nicely, me hearty wench."

"Not so much of the wench," laughed Peggy.

She returned with a plate of her biscuits and handed them to the pirate.

"How much do you want for that stowaway?" asked the captain, pointing his sword at Zed.

"He's not for sale," shouted Tim from the stern. "You can have the serving wench, though, at a cheap price."

Peggy shook her fist at Tim.

"I'm not for sale, either."

As the pirate with the ship's biscuits jumped back on his boat, he put his hat with the skull and crossbones onto Zed's head and the captain threw him his plastic sword.

"See you on Treasure Island. We always need new members for our crew."

As the stern of their boat passed Tim, a pirate threw a pack of four beer cans at him.

"Ah ee," he screeched, "got these from the last

boat we boarded."

Tim looked behind as their boat zigzagged down the canal. Zed jumped onto the roof with his new pirate's hat and sword.

"Let's board the next boat we see, Tim."

"Aye, aye, captain."

It was early evening when Tim decided to stop for the night. He took the power off the engine with the throttle and glided Kingfisher into the bank. They had made good time and were now only a few hours from Boswell's Yard. There were no mooring rings, so Tim and Peggy banged in long metal spikes with a club hammer to hold the lines. Peggy cut a blue plastic bottle in half and asked Zed to put a piece on top of each spike in case a walker or cyclist went into them. Zed pulled up the engine stop and turned the ignition key off. "Very good," said Tim. "What do we do now?"

Zed thought for a moment. "Turn the stern gland."

"Well done."

Tim removed the engine cover and gave it a clockwise turn.

Tim asked Zed to take Barney for a walk while he got the fishing rods set up. Zed and Barney ran along the towpath, and then disappeared into the thick woodland. Tim often moored here when he had groups on board his community boats Odin and Thor. There was a small, grassed area where they could pitch tents and light a fire. Across the canal was a park with an outdoor swimming pool, which was called a lido. This was always popular, as many youngsters had never swum before in an outdoor pool. The woods were also rich in wildlife, which was one of Tim's hobbies. He liked nothing better than sharing this knowledge with other people, particularly youngsters whom he hoped might develop an interest in the countryside.

When Zed and Barney returned from their walk, Tim had already set up two fishing rods and placed them on stands at the edge of the canal.

"You were a long time."

"We got a bit lost and ended up on the other side of the wood, and we met a man who knew Barney. He said he knew you, too."

"What man? "

"He said his name was Smokey."

"Ah, Smokey Joe, he's harmless enough."

"He had a really long beard and an old coat. Is he a tramp?"

"Sort of, he lives in an old caravan on the edge of the wood. He's been there for years. Some people say he fought in the war in Iraq and then cracked up when he came home. It's a long story. Anyway, are you ready to fish?"

"Yeah. Bet I catch more than you," said Zed, picking up a rod.

"You can put your own bait on," laughed Tim,

handing him a tub of wriggling maggots.

They sat in the evening sun, watching their floats resting on the still water. Tim could never really work out the fascination of watching a float and waiting for that moment when it suddenly disappeared beneath the water. It was the same hypnotic feeling as when you sit staring into a camp-fire, watching the flames as they dance around the burning wood making shapes and faces.

Peggy had put a chicken in the oven to roast and then walked over the bridge to the park. It was a steep walk up the hill to the lido. Beyond it were two large iron gates that led out of the park and onto the main road that ran through the village where she had once lived as a girl. She turned left out of the gates and into the small cemetery that was hidden behind a tall red brick wall. Following the gravel footpath, she came to a grassed area where small neat graves with white headstones and wooden crosses nestled under the branches of an old oak tree. She knelt in front of the one with a statue of an angel cradling a child in its arms. On the stone, it read, "David Hickman, aged five days." It was Peggy's son. Only her parents had known about it and they were no longer alive. Peggy and Karl had met when he was working at the circus that came every year to the park with the lido. They had both been 18 years old. Forty-two years ago. She had become pregnant. The circus had moved on and with it, Karl. Such was the hurt that it would be her first and last relationship. She spent a few minutes alone talking to David, then left the cemetery and walked back through the iron gates into the park. The lido was closed and the sun was falling below the horizon. It would soon be dark. Tim and Zed must be starving, she thought. When she arrived back at the boat, they were both still sitting staring at the little yellow floats bobbing on the surface of the water.

"Good walk?" asked Tim.

"Good walk," she replied.

That night over the roast chicken, there was much talk between Tim and Zed of the fish that got away. "I'm just glad that I didn't depend on you to catch the dinner, or we would all starve," laughed Peggy. After dinner, they sat around the fire that Tim and Zed had built earlier, whilst waiting for that prize fish that never came. It was just off the towpath in a small clearing. Tim had asked Zed to find some small sticks, which he called "kindling." They had to be very dry and preferably from above the ground, in the branches and bushes. Once they had a small stock, Tim showed Zed how to gather some burning woods and logs. He pushed a large stick into the ground, and using some of the kindling, made a shape like a wigwam tent. He packed the inside tightly with dry grass and bark from a tree, so the flames would catch all of the kindling. He flicked his lighter and held it close to the dry grass. When the kindling was well lit, he laid some burning wood in a criss-cross fashion over the fire.

"When this starts to burn through, we can add some of our logs," he said. "This sort of fire settles well and will give us a lot of hot embers to cook on."

"Do you always carry that?" Zed asked pointing to the Swiss Army knife that Tim had used to sharpen the stick to build the fire around.

"I do, but you remember, young man, that a knife is a tool and like all tools, you have to learn how to use it properly and how look after it." He told Zed that when out on Odin and Thor, he carried four cutting tools: a knife, a bow saw, a hand axe and a felling axe – and he never allowed anyone else to use them.

Peggy sat wrapped in her old camp blanket. She had kept it since her days as a youth leader. It was covered in lots of badges from the many places that she had travelled to. Zed lay on the ground with Barney, poking a long stick into the flames, and then making shapes in the dark with the burning end. Tim would occasionally kick a falling log back into the fire. They stayed until the fire had become a small bed of glowing red embers and the darkness had closed in on them. Zed had fallen fast asleep on the ground. Tim told Peggy not to wake him and picked him up instead, carrying him to the boat. He put him on the bed and covered him with the duvet.

"Goodnight, little stowaway," he said, closing the door.

After Peggy went to bed, Tim soaked the fire with

two buckets of water from the canal and then poured himself a small drink from his hip flask. He sat for a long time, looking up at the black sparkling sky. This was the only time he ever wondered about the existence of God.

A bold bright light woke Peggy on Wednesday morning. She hadn't slept well and closed her eyes once more to shut out the light. It was six o'clock, and she felt a strange sadness in the pit of her tummy. This trip had reminded her too much of being on board Turtle, and it was also the last day they would spend with Zed. Opening her eyes, she watched a small spider descending on a thin strand of web. It reminded her of the one time she had been persuaded to go abseiling at Toad Rocks – never again. She had no head for heights.

She didn't mind spiders. It was the mosquitoes she hated and there were plenty of them on the canals. She lay for a long time, looking up at the curved cream roof of the cabin, imagining that it was a blank canvas and that she had her oil paints and brushes with her. She would paint the story of her three days on Kingfisher, her thoughts and feelings and the fun it had been. It would remain there forever, so people could look at it on their last day aboard the boat.

Tim knocked on the door.

"Rise and shine. Nice cup of tea for you." It was her favourite, Earl Grey.

"Sleep well?"

"Not really."

"Nor me," said Tim. "Strange. I normally sleep well on a boat."

"Is Zed awake?"

"No, he's still fast asleep."

"How long will it be before we get to Boswell's Yard?"

"About three hours. Don't rush – I'll cook breakfast."

"OK. I won't be long."

When Zed woke, Barney was asleep next to him, his head resting on the pillow. He wondered what dogs dreamed about.

"Barney, are you awake?"

He opened one eye and gave a brief wag of his tail.

"You are a lazy dog."

He climbed out of bed and drew back the curtain. An early morning mist was hovering just above the surface of the still water. On the far side of the canal, a tall reed bed blew gently in the breeze and two cygnets, baby swans, their young feathers still a light grey colour, were looking up at him in anticipation of some bread. Remaining still for some time, he looked at the view from the window, then down at his new red and white trainers, and across at Barney, now curled in a ball. He picked up the two yellow floats that Tim had given him to remember their fishing trip. When he looked out of the window again, the little cygnets had been joined by two beautiful white swans. He watched as the family swam gently away before disappearing into the morning mist.

"You up, Zed? Want some breakfast?"

At the sound of Tim's voice, Barney leaped from the bed.

After breakfast, while Tim was doing the engine checks, Zed polished the brass tiller bar and pin and the roof vents.

"'Ow often do you go out on your boats, Tim?"

"Do you mean Odin and Thor?"

"Yeah, them camping ones you was telling me about last night when we was fishing."

"It depends when a group books them out, but it can be up to 20 times a year."

"Where are they kept?

"Well, you know where you sneaked on board this boat by the canal shop? They're moored near there, just up from my cottage."

"Will I be able to go on them one day?"

What could Tim say? He didn't even know if they would see Zed any more after today. He scuffed up Zed's red hair with his large, rough hand.

"I'm sure you will one day, boy, I'm sure you will."

Zed put the polished tiller bar back on.

"Very good," said Tim, "now you can see your face in it." He laughed, "Not that you'd want to, did you comb your hair this morning?"

"I 'ain't got a comb."

Tim pulled one from his back pocket. "You can keep that."

Before leaving the mooring, Tim tidied the area where the fire had been and asked Zed to stack the unused logs they had collected at the base of a tree. He told Zed that the only thing you ever leave in the countryside is your thanks.

"Have you ever been camping, Zed?" he asked.

"What – you mean in a tent?"

Tim chuckled. "Well, that's what most people go camping in."

"No, never. I'd like to, though."

After letting the bow and stern lines go, Tim gave the stern a big push away from the bank. Then Peggy did the same to the bow.

"Why do we push the stern off first, Zed?"

"So the boat won't bang on the side as we pull away."

"Well done. Now you can steer while I get a cuppa."

CHAPTER FOUR:

The Journey to South London

On Wednesday morning, Janice Phillips had driven the five miles from the village to the main railway station in the town. She had phoned Zed's Gran from the school on Tuesday afternoon and had spent a long time explaining what had happened to Zed and arranging her visit to London.

Parking her car in the pay-and-display car park she went to the ticket office to collect her tickets. The journey to Paddington Station in London would take about two hours. Standing on the platform, she looked out over the small town. The tall spire of St. Stephen's church dominated the skyline. Below it was the square, where the market would already be very busy. People came from all over the county to buy from the many different stalls and then meet friends for lunch in the pubs and restaurants. On Friday, they had a different kind of market, when farmers brought along their livestock to sell. The children from St. Mark's School loved coming to this cattle market, and several times a year, their teachers would organise trips so the children could learn all about farming and how to care for animals. Many of the children came from farming families, and so had a good understanding of what to do. But others, in particular those that had moved into the village from the cities, had very little idea of where their meat came from or how it got into the shops.

Suddenly, the overhead loudspeaker burst into life. "The train for London Paddington will be arriving at platform three in five minutes." All the people on the platform started to move closer to the edge so that they could get a seat. Janice had a reservation: carriage four, seat six. As the train stopped, the automatic doors unlocked and people spilled out onto the platform. They were all going to the market. She found her seat and soon the train was moving out of the station.

The train ran alongside the canal and passed over the bridge that Peggy had gone under in Kingfisher two days earlier. As Janice looked out of the window, the fields and woods passed by in a blur as the train gathered speed. She was not really looking forward to finding her way across London to Rotherhithe. Everything had seemed so fast and busy when she last visited and she had been glad to get back home to the country. She was surprised how much of the canal followed the railway line. She kept catching glimpses of it all the way to Reading. It wasn't long before the conductor announced that they would soon be arriving at London Paddington. Her journey had taken just over two hours. She remembered Tim and Peggy telling her that to travel the same distance along the Kennet and Avon Canal and River Thames by narrow boat would take five days.

Stepping from the train onto platform one at Paddington Station, she looked up at the huge, glazed roof, supported by wrought iron arches. "What a wonderful building," she thought. What it must have been like in the days of steam engines when the noise and the great clouds of grey steam would fill the arches and hang underneath the domed roof! Janice passed the statue of Isambard Kingdom Brunel, who had designed the station in 1854. She thought that this would make a wonderful history project for the

Year Six children at her school. She decided to arrange a day trip when she got back. The entrance to the underground station was just behind the Paddington Bear stall. A woman wearing a blue sash was giving away free bottles of water at the top of the steps. Janice took one and stepped onto the downward escalator. At the bottom, two British Transport policemen – one holding a brown and white Springer spaniel – were keenly watching the coming and going of the crowds. She wondered if they were checking for explosives or drugs. A policewoman was searching the bag of a young man with long hair and pink jeans and a guitar slung over his shoulder. She saw the queue for the ticket office, which snaked in between a metal pen. It reminded her of the sheep waiting to be dipped on the farm.

Janice had to make two attempts at crossing the busy floor, as the first time, she was carried along by the tide of people coming from the underground and making their way up to the main line station. Joining the queue at the ticket office, she took the piece of paper from her bag on which she had written the journey details that her secretary had given her. An automated female voice called: "cashier number four, please." She did as requested and walked to the window.

"Good morning."

There was a grunt from the man behind the glass.

"Where to?"

Slightly taken aback by the man's rudeness, she asked for a return ticket to Rotherhithe.

"Three pounds twenty," he said, throwing the tickets into a plastic revolving tray. She dropped in a five-pound note and her tickets came back in return with her change. She didn't attempt to say 'thank you'. "Welcome to London," she thought.

Checking her small underground route map, she made her way towards the Circle Line for Westminster, where she would change to the Jubilee Line for London Bridge. She then had to catch an overland train to South Bermondsey. It surprised her how many people were begging for money around the stations. One woman was sitting at the bottom of some steps, holding a baby, not saying anything – just staring, with an outstretched hand. In one of the connecting tunnels, there was a busker playing blues music on a saxophone. He was very good, so Janice stopped to listen and then dropped a pound into his box.

The underground trains were packed and she thought how hot and miserable everyone looked. "How do they do this every day?" she wondered.

It didn't take long for the overground train to travel from London Bridge to South Bermondsey. It was an old station, with wooden platforms and buildings. Once again, Janice found the piece of paper that she had written the directions on. "When you leave the station, go past the travellers' site on the

63

left, follow the path to the main road, and then turn right. When you reach the George pub, turn right. That is the entrance to the estate. The Nelson block of flats is the second one on the left after the parade of shops." It took her 15 minutes to walk.

The main road was clogged with traffic and she had a narrow escape when the back wheels of a long red bendy bus ran over the pavement, near to where she was standing. But it was the noise that she found the worst – and why were there so many ambulances, all making that loud screeching noise that went right through you? When she reached the entrance to the estate, she looked up at the four tall tower blocks in front of her. She noticed some flowers tied to a lamp post and school blazers and ties hanging on the railings. Pinned to a tree, there was a picture of a young black lad smiling at the camera. Underneath there were candles in small jars and more flowers.

Mrs. Hawkins, Zed's Gran, had been up since six o'clock that morning. Ever since she had received Janice Phillips' phone call about Zed, she had been worried about her forthcoming visit. She loved Zed dearly and had looked after him ever since he was born. Her daughter Amanda had only been 16 at the time and she had no idea how to care for a baby. Gran never knew the father. Even Amanda barely knew him. Gran's own husband had walked out on her when the two children, Amanda and Darren, were very young. She had taken a job in a factory in the

East End of London. The hours were long but it was the only way she could pay the rent for the flat and feed and clothe the children. Her next-door neighbour would look after them until she arrived home. But she was in competition with the bad people that lived on the same estate, and no amount of hard work or care by Gran was going to prevent Amanda and Darren from falling into the hands of the villains that lived in the area.

Mrs. Hawkins had known since he was at junior school that Darren had behavioural problems. Although he had been given lots of help by the teachers, it did no good. He was eventually suspended and then permanently excluded from school. At his comprehensive, the same had happened in Year Nine and he was sent to a children's centre for five mornings a week.

When he was 14, he had pushed Gran against the kitchen wall because she had tried to stop him going out. Several times the police had to be called and had taken him to the station to calm down, often in handcuffs. Social workers suggested to Gran that he should be put into care for his own good and her safety but she wouldn't hear of it. "He can be very good and considerate," she would say, and he could. Like the time he had given her a large bunch of flowers for her birthday. Then she discovered that he had stolen them from the crematorium. Still, it was the thought that counted. But his demon temper was always bubbling just below the surface and at the slightest provocation, he would lose it completely. When he was 21, he was arrested for driving a car without insurance or a licence and as it was his second offence, he was sent to prison for six months. After coming out of prison, he had a few jobs labouring on building sites and then met a man in a pub who offered him a job working for the circus. He seemed to settle down and enjoyed travelling around the country. Gran was happy that at least he wasn't getting into trouble and was away from the estate.

The estate that Nelson Block was on wasn't as big as some of the housing estates in London. There were four high-rise blocks with 10 floors in each block. They were surrounded by maisonettes with two floors in each. Built in the 1960s, in dull grey brickwork, all of the buildings seemed to merge into one blob of concrete. Each block had a small car park, which more often than not had dumped cars in it. The fire brigade were often called to extinguish the fires that kids had lit in the cars. The police were always on hand to stop the firemen being pelted with stones. There was a green open space in the middle of the estate with broken seats and the remains of a children's playground. The shops in the small parade were all closed now, apart from the newsagent and one used as a base for the Police Community Support Officers.

Gran's flat was on the eighth floor of Nelson

House. It had three small bedrooms, a sitting room, a kitchen and a toilet with a bath. The paintwork was dull and grubby and the wallpaper was peeling. Very often, Gran would have to walk all the way up the stairs from the ground floor, as the lift was out of order. When it was working, she didn't like going in it, either, as some people used it as a toilet. Graffiti tags covered the walls of the corridors and stairways.

The entrance to Nelson House was through a heavy blue locked door that could only be opened by punching a code into a keypad. Janice Phillips put in the numbers two, four and seven that Gran had given her over the telephone. The door opened with a loud click. Inside, she pressed the green button to call the lift. After a couple of minutes, the doors to the small metal box separated and as she stepped in, she could smell recently used disinfectant. The lift slowly moved up to the eighth floor, rocking gently from side to side. There was a red button to press in case of an emergency. She hoped there wouldn't be one. Stepping out onto the balcony, she was struck by the magnificent view across London. She could see Tower Bridge and St Paul's Cathedral.

The door to number 35 was slightly ajar as she rang the doorbell. Gran opened it fully.

"Hello, Mrs. Hawkins, I'm Janice Phillips, nice to meet you."

They shook hands and Gran showed Janice into the small sitting room. The furniture was old, but it was clean and tidy. Gran was already nervous and worried about what was going to happen to Zed.

"Would you like a cup of tea?" she asked.

"I could murder one after that journey, thank you."

Gran smiled and went into the kitchen. Janice Phillips noticed a framed picture of two children that she thought must be Darren and Amanda, and another of Amanda pushing a baby in a pram that she assumed was Zed.

After they had finished their tea and biscuits, Janice told Gran everything that had happened to Zed since he had run away from the circus and about Peggy and Tim. Gran explained through her tears that when Zed was excluded from his junior school and Amanda sent to prison, she felt it would be best for Zed to go and stay with Darren in the circus. She wanted to get him away from the estate and the area. She was shocked when Janice explained that Darren hadn't been looking after him and hadn't even reported him missing when he had run away.

Gran shook her head. "'Is own nephew. 'Ow could 'e treat 'im like that?"

"Has Zed been to see his mum in prison?" said Janice.

"'E wanted to, but Amanda said no. She didn't want 'im to see 'er in that place. I visit 'er once a month. So what 'appens now?" asked Gran.

"Well, the first thing is, you need to speak to Zed

on the phone to reassure him. He's more worried about you than he is about himself." Janice took a mobile phone from her handbag and dialled Peggy's number.

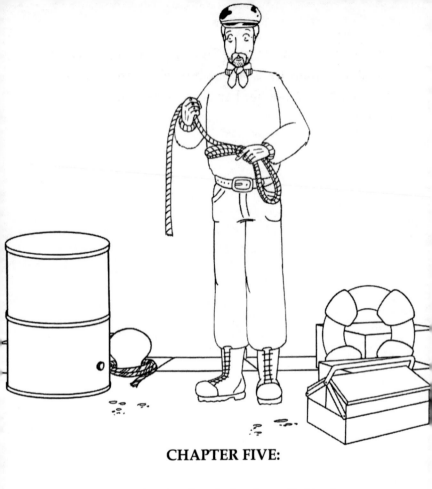

CHAPTER FIVE:

Destination Reached – Boswells Yard

It was the middle of the afternoon when Tim steered Kingfisher through the narrow entrance into Boswell's boat yard. The day had passed quickly, even though one of the locks had had a broken paddle and it took a long time to fill up. Peggy and Zed were down below, cleaning through the boat and putting all the unused food into carrier bags.

"Peggy," called Zed, "Is that your phone ringing?"

She looked around the galley to see where the tone was coming from. She was always losing it. Taking the phone from under a tea towel next to the sink, she pressed the green button.

"Hello."

"Hi Peggy, it's Janice. I'm here in London with Zed's Gran. Could you put him on? She'd like to speak to him."

Peggy handed the phone to Zed. "It's your Gran, love."

Zed took the phone. Peggy touched him on the arm. "Be back in a minute." It was a good 10 minutes before Zed came up onto the stern of the boat with the phone and handed it back to Peggy. His eyes were red and his cheeks damp from tears.

"You alright, love?"

He nodded and went back inside the boat.

"Leave him, it's for the best," said Tim.

Tim had moored Kingfisher near to the dry dock and next to the diesel pump, where boats would stop to refuel. Even Jack Boswell would admit that his boatyard was a bit of a tip. There was almost the same number of old cars in the yard as boats. Although Jack said he liked restoring them back to their original condition, some of them hadn't been touched for years, although Jack did occasionally sell parts to collectors.

71

On the side of the basin was a rusting old lorry with a crane on the back. Jack would use this to lift boats out of the water and into the yard. They would then be lowered onto big wooden sleepers, so they could be worked on. At one end of the yard was an area covered with a black tin roof. This was the entrance to the workshop. There was a pile of old engines and a rack with some outboard motors on it, a big mobile generator and a stack of sheet steel for repairing boats. At the side was a kennel for Rex, Jack's German shepherd, who was attached to a long chain. At night, when the gates were locked, Rex would be let loose to patrol the yard.

Tim told Zed that the boats standing on the wooden sleepers were there to have the bottom cleaned and painted. "It's best to have them done every couple of years," he said. "You can also check the hull for any rusting or thinning of the steel." He asked Zed to tell him what the hull was.

"The bottom of the boat," Zed replied.

"Well done."

They stood next to the dry dock. It was deep and empty.

"It works just like a lock," explained Tim. "Open the paddles to fill it, then steer the boat in. You then close the gates and paddles and pump out the water. You have to make sure that the boat rests on the supports as the water drains out, then you can work on it."

Gran had told Zed that Mrs. Phillips had arranged for him to stay with her family that night and that Tim and Peggy would take him to the house on their way home. On Thursday morning, Derek Phillips, her husband, would take him to Paddington Station, where Gran would meet him. Zed had asked Gran if he could stay the night with Tim and Peggy but Mrs. Phillips had said that was not possible. Gran had also told Zed that they had a son and daughter the same age as him, so he could play with them.

Tim walked to the old mobile caravan that Jack Boswell used as an office and home. He had known him for years.

"Morning, Jack," he said. "I see your filing system hasn't improved."

Jack was sitting behind a large wooden desk. The top of it was completely covered in sheets of paper, old envelopes and a large stack of yellow wallet folders. They were all covered in oily fingerprints. On the floor beside the desk was an overflowing waste paper basket surrounded by used plastic cups and rolled up pieces of paper.

"How you doing, Tim?" he said. "I didn't know you were bringing the boat up."

"I wasn't. It's a long story. Can I use the phone to call a taxi to the station?"

"Sure, my friend," said Jack. "It's under this lot somewhere."

The taxi took about 40 minutes to arrive. They

had moved all of their bags from the boat and onto the grass next to the car parking area. The driver was not impressed by the deep holes in Jack's driveway.

As they drove away, Zed looked out of the back window at Kingfisher tied to the wooden jetty. He gave a small wave.

"Goodbye, little boat."

Peggy put her arm around his shoulders. The driver asked about their trip, told Zed he was lucky to have parents who took him on boat trips and moaned about it being too hot. Nobody was really listening but Tim felt obliged to reply, as he was sitting in the front seat. When they reached the station, Tim paid the fare and they walked to the platform. Although it had taken nearly three days by boat, the train journey back would only be about an hour. They watched as the scenery flashed by in between stations, taking them nearer to the place where they would have to say goodbye to Zed. Barney loved boats, but hated buses and trains and lay sulking at Tim's feet.

The train slowed as it crossed the bridge over the canal before arriving at the station. Zed looked down on the narrow boats moored on either side of the canal before it disappeared behind a large warehouse. There was a loud screeching of metal as the train went over the points and ran alongside the platform. Zed closed his eyes, hoping it would keep going. Then, with a shudder, it stopped. The automatic doors opened and Barney leaped onto the platform with little regard for those people waiting to get on.

Outside the station, they boarded the number nine bus that would take them the five miles to the village. Tim and Peggy knew several people on the bus, all of whom wanted to know more about Zed than they wanted to tell them. This was the only problem with living in the countryside: everyone knew everyone else and their business. There were no bus stops en route. People just stood on the side of the road and waved the bus down. They would then spend a long time talking to the driver before sitting down. "No wonder it never runs on time," thought Tim. Barney lay in the aisle and yelped when one old man put his walking stick down on his tail.

After passing through several villages, the bus stopped outside St. Mark's Church. The Phillips family lived in one of the new houses at the end of the village. Tim and Peggy remembered the uproar from the residents when planning permission had been given to build them. But in the end, everyone had to admit they had done a good job with the little close of 12 houses. They walked slowly. Zed put his hand in Peggy's. All the houses in the close had large open lawns with driveways and were built in a buff-coloured square stone. Number four, the Phillips's house, was the second one on the left, with red and blue balloons tied to the porch.

Tim knocked. The door opened and a tall, thin man, wearing a baseball cap and grey tracksuit, opened the door. It was Derek Phillips.

"Hello all," he said, "do come in. This must be Zed?"

They went into the dining room, which overlooked a long back garden. Soon, the two children who had been playing volleyball came into the house and stood next to their father.

"Emma, Luke, this is Zed. He's the same age as you."

"We were 12 yesterday," said Emma. "Are you 12?"

"No, I'm still 11," said Zed.

"Do you like playing volleyball, Zed?" asked Mr. Phillips.

"Never played it before," he replied, shrugging his shoulders.

"Why not have a go?"

Zed reluctantly followed Emma and Luke into the garden, followed by Barney.

Derek made some tea for Tim and Peggy and they sat for some time talking about Zed, his Gran and the boat trip. Derek said he had never been on a narrow boat before and that it sounded like fun. He would have to ring Harry Martin at the boatyard about hiring one for a family holiday. Tim invited him to come and look over Odin and Thor.

"I suppose we should be making a move," said Peggy, finishing her cup of tea. Peggy and Tim had been rehearsing this moment in their minds for a long time. Derek called the children in from the garden. Tim spoke to Zed first.

"Well, mate," he said, "we need to be off now."

He placed his large hand gently on Zed's head.

"You be a good lad, now."

Peggy didn't say anything. She couldn't. They hugged and Zed held Peggy tightly around the waist. "You'll be fine," she told him, "and you'll see your Gran tomorrow."

"But I want to stay with you. I don't want to go back to London. I'll never see you again," Zed sobbed. Tim bent down so he was looking directly into Zed's face. He put both his hands on Zed's shaking shoulders.

"Listen, boy, you remember just how much fun you've had, and I'm sure you will see us again one day."

When they reached the bottom of the close, they turned to wave. Barney barked. Emma had her arm around Zed.

By the time Janice returned from London, the children were in bed. Derek had put a camp bed in Luke's room for Zed to sleep on. Luke had asked if they could sleep in his tent in the garden but Mr. and Mrs. Philips wanted to keep an eye on Zed overnight. Before they went to sleep, Luke showed Zed how to play some computer games and Emma came in to say goodnight. She gave him a kiss and he blushed. Before they went to bed, Janice and Derek looked in to check that the boys were all right. Luke was fast asleep and Zed was very still with his eyes closed. He wasn't asleep, though. When Derek and Janice had left the room, he opened his eyes and lay for a long time staring up at the ceiling. He put his hand out, but Barney wasn't next to him.

Derek Phillips woke at six o'clock in the morning, showered and dressed. He worked as a surveyor for a building company in Swindon and would always catch the one-minute-past-eight train. Today, he had arranged to take the morning off work, so that he could take Zed to London, where Gran would meet him at Paddington Station. He drank a cup of coffee, and then went to Luke's room to wake the boys up. He drew the curtains to let some light into the room. Luke was still fast asleep, but Zed's bed was empty. His bag had gone and so had he. Derek went back into his bedroom and woke his wife. When they went downstairs, they noticed the back door was unlocked. Janice rang Tim's number. It was ten minutes past seven. Barney heard the phone and started barking. It woke Tim.

"Hello."

"Tim, its Janice. Zed's gone. He's run away."

"Damn," said Tim, "that's all we need."

Janice said that she would call in on Tim on her way to work. He said he would ring Peggy and get her to come over. Janice arrived at Tim's cottage on the side of the canal just after eight o'clock. Peggy had come straight over from her flat in the village after Tim had phoned her.

"He could be anywhere, poor little mite," she said, "we'll have to contact the police."

"Well, he certainly wouldn't have gone back to the circus or to London," said Tim. "You go to work, Janice, let me and Peggy see if we can find him."

They agreed that if they hadn't found Zed by the middle of the day, then they would contact the police. Janice Phillips said that she would ring Gran when she got to work and tell her what had happened.

Opposite Tim's cottage, on the other side of the canal, was a magnificent tall beech tree. Tim would often sit outside, watching the tallest of the branches blowing in the wind. Occasionally, he would follow the white vapour trail of a passing jet high in the blue sky. He would watch until the firm, slim line turned into white puffy balls. This helped him to concentrate. Peggy sat quietly, brushing the loose hair from Barney's black and white coat. There was nothing else to do but think. There were no leads to follow, or calls to make. All they could do was go over the events and conversations of the past three days for any clue that could lead to Zed's whereabouts. They both felt, though, that he wouldn't be far from the canal.

There was a sudden crack as the wind got under a plastic sheet that was covering a pile of logs that Tim had stored for the winter. Tim watched for a long time as it flapped and heaved at the corner ties holding it down.

"I know where he is, Peggy," he shouted.

"What do you mean, where?"

She stopped brushing Barney and jumped up.

"How do you know?"

"I just do," said Tim. "Trust me. He's on the camper boats. He's on Odin or Thor. That's where he'll be hiding."

They walked quickly along the towpath towards where the two boats were moored. Barney ran ahead, as he always did. It had rained in the night and the holes in the path had filled with water, which sloshed around Peggy's feet in her open sandals. When Barney reached the boats, he stood with his tail wagging and barking. Tim realised straight away that someone had been on the boats, as two of the thick rubber loops that secured the canvas to the cleats on the gunwales were undone. He unclipped another two and pulled up the long zip. He lifted Barney up and climbed up behind him. Barney ran through the galley area towards the rows of bunks at the front of the boat. His excited barking told Tim all he needed to know. Zed was sitting on the edge of one of the top bunks. He said nothing as Tim approached. He just stared down at the floor. Tim bent down and lifted Barney on to the bunk beside him. Zed looked up and put his arm round Barney's neck. Barney licked his face, happy to see his young friend once again.

Peggy had now joined Tim and they both stood either side of Zed.

"Well, young man, you've led us a right little dance," said Peggy.

"Sorry, Peggy. Sorry, Tim." His eyes dropped to the floor again. Tim put his hand under Zed's chin and lifted up his head."

"Well, we're just very glad that you came here. At least you're safe and we've found you. Come on."

He lifted Zed off the bunk, followed by Barney. Peggy put her arm around Zed.

"You had me really worried," she said, "really worried, and don't you say sorry again or I'll throw you overboard."

Zed smiled and they all went off the boat and onto the towpath.

CHAPTER SIX:

The Deal

Back at Tim's cottage, Peggy insisted that Zed had a bath while she cooked him some breakfast. Tim phoned Janice to let her know that he had been found. Janice said that she would call round after school had finished, at half past three. Zed was worried about this, as he didn't know what he would say to her or

Derek, and worse, he still had to explain to Gran why he had run away from their house.

Before Peggy had phoned Tim on Monday, he had been working on the engine of a narrow boat called Spirit. This was one of a number of boats that Tim serviced and repaired each year. The owners would moor the boats outside Tim's cottage, so he was near to his little wooden workshop that stood next door. He needed to get this boat finished, as he had another one booked in for Saturday. After they had eaten lunch, Peggy emptied Zed's bag and threw the contents into the washing machine. Tim had changed into a pair of dark blue oily overalls and his heavy leather boots. He threw a small pair of overalls at Zed. "Here," he said, "put these on. They were left by a lad doing work experience last month." Even though they were a small size, Zed was lost inside them. Tim bent down and rolled up the sleeves and legs. "There we are, just fine," he said, laughing.

"What do I need these for?"

"Because, Mister, you are going to help me and learn a little bit about boat engines at the same time. Then we'll sort out what's happening to you when Mrs. Phillips arrives."

Zed nodded. "OK."

"Haven't you forgotten something, young man?" said Peggy, holding out her mobile phone.

Zed took the phone and dialled Gran's number. She did most of the talking. "Yeah Gran, no Gran, sorry Gran," he said, then handed the phone to Peggy.

"Come on," said Tim and they went outside to where the narrow boat Spirit was moored. On the towpath beside the stern of the boat was a large blue metal tool kit. Tim stepped on board and lifted the engine cover, then jumped down into the compartment beside the engine.

He asked Zed to open up the lid of the tool kit.

Zed pulled it apart and saw two trays full of screws and bolts, hinges and metal pins. The bottom part was full up with screwdrivers and spanners, pincers and pliers and two big hammers. For the next two hours, Tim worked on the engine. Zed would pass him each tool when it was needed. Sometimes he would mix up the spanner and screwdriver sizes. Tim would occasionally stop and explain to Zed what he was doing and show him the parts he was changing or cleaning. Before putting the tools back in the toolkit, Zed would have to wipe the oil and grease off with tissue taken from a big roll. He liked having his hands all oily and black, as this made him look like Tim.

Peggy and Gran had a long chat on the mobile phone. They were both concerned that if they tried to force Zed to go back to London, he might run away again. Gran said she was pleased that Zed felt so happy in the countryside and understood why he didn't want to come back to London, but there was no other choice and she had to try to get him back into school.

"When are the school holidays?" asked Peggy.

"I got no idea," said Gran, "but it must be soon."

Peggy said she wanted to discuss something with Tim and Janice and asked Gran if it would be all right to ring her back later that evening.

Tim replaced the engine cover on Spirit and picked up the heavy tool kit. He pointed to a plastic box with the old parts that he had replaced in the engine.

"Can you carry that, Zed?"

Zed picked up the box and followed Tim to the wooden shed. Tim took a tin from the shelf and opened it.

"Hold out your hand, Zed."

He dropped a small lump of slimy green goo in his palm.

"Now rub your hands together and it will clean all the oil and grease off. Then go and wash them under the tap outside."

Tim did the same. Zed liked the feeling as the goo squished between his fingers.

When Tim and Zed went back to the cottage, Janice had already arrived and was sitting talking to Peggy. Zed looked nervous when he saw her. She smiled.

"How are you, Zed? she asked. "I hear you've been learning about boat engines."

Zed relaxed when he realised she wasn't going to tell him off. Tim passed him a glass of cola and they all sat down together.

"Zed, love," said Peggy, "I want you to go and play with Barney in the garden while we have a little chat about things. Is that OK?"

"Yeah, sure. Come on, Barney."

"Don't go away," called Peggy. "I won't," said Zed. "I promise."

After talking to Gran on the phone, he knew he had to be good and go back to live in London.

Peggy spoke to Tim and Janice and outlined her plan. At first, Tim thought she was mad. Janice Phillips was concerned that they didn't really know Zed that well and they could be putting themselves at risk.

"Where will he stay?" asked Tim.

"With you," replied Peggy. "I could move in as well, you've got two spare rooms."

Tim was not convinced. "Look, Peggy, I think he's a great little lad, but...."

Peggy interrupted him.

"The schools are breaking up soon for six weeks. We could do a lot for him in that time. Then he could go back in September for the new term."

"What if they can't get him into school?" said Tim.

"Maybe I could help with that," replied Janice.

"Come on, Tim," said Peggy. "He could help you with the boats and maybe we can stop him turning out like his uncle."

Tim turned to Janice.

"What do you think?"

She thought for a moment.

"I think that if his Gran agrees, it's worth trying. Peggy has a point. If nobody does anything and he goes back to that estate, he will end up like Darren or worse."

Tim nodded.

"OK, then. It will be good to have an apprentice."

Peggy smiled. "Thanks, Tim."

Before they called Zed in from the garden, Peggy phoned Gran. At first, she wouldn't hear of their suggestion, saying that it wasn't fair to offload her responsibility onto them. Peggy slowly explained the plan and that Janice Phillips was going to help her to get Zed back into school in September. She also suggested that Gran come down to stay for a couple of weekends. In the end, she agreed, but only on the understanding that she sent enough money for Zed's keep and to buy him some new clothes. Peggy didn't want it but there was no point in arguing. She told Gran that she would get Zed to ring her that evening.

Tim called Zed in from the garden. He sat on the sofa with Barney. Tim had given up trying to keep Barney off the furniture. Zed expected to be told he was going back to London either today or tomorrow.

"Zed," said Peggy. "How would you like to spend the school holidays here with us?"

Zed looked at Tim, then at Janice Phillips. He said nothing. Peggy was just about to repeat the question when he put his arm round Barney's neck and tears started to run down his cheeks.

"I thought I 'ad to go back to London," he sobbed. "Can I really stay 'ere?"

"You can," replied Tim. "But any nonsense and you will be keel hauled."

"What's that?"

Peggy interrupted.

"Don't ask, love. There is one condition, though. In September, when you go back to school in London, you behave. Do we have a deal?" He ran across to Peggy and threw his arms around her.

"Deal," he said.

Janice ran Peggy back to the village to pick up some of her clothes and a sleeping bag for Zed. Tim and Zed cleared a load of old boxes and junk from the small spare room. Most were books that Tim had read over the years and had always meant to throw out but never did. By the time Peggy returned, the room looked almost clean. There was a bed, a wardrobe, a chest of drawers with a cracked mirror and a blue carpet that was pretty worn. Tim opened the windows.

"It's not really decorated as a kid's room," he said. "Maybe we can get some posters for the wall. What football team do you support, Zed?"

"Dunno really. Millwall, I suppose."

"Well I'm sure we can find something you like in town. Now, you need to ring your Gran."

That night after dinner, Peggy watched her soaps. She had brought her portable television with her. Tim did not have a television and she wasn't going to miss her weekly programmes. Tim sat in the kitchen listening to the radio and Zed played with Barney on the grass by the canal. After Peggy and Zed had gone to bed, Tim sat outside and studied the sparkling night sky. He watched a shooting star falling earthwards and named it Zed.

The following day, Peggy took Zed into town. The owner of Spirit was coming to pick up his boat after the service on the engine and Tim had promised Harry Martin that he would help him put a new window in one of his hire boats. The tiller bar from another boat had gone through the glass while it was in a lock. By the time Tim got back to the cottage, Peggy and Zed had unpacked the shopping. Zed had some new clothes and posters for his room. He had chosen animals in the wild. Tim made a cup of tea and fell onto the sofa.

"Don't forget we've got that youth group coming on Sunday, Peg. We'll have to get the boats ready tomorrow."

"Does that mean we'll be going on the camper boats?" called Zed from his room.

"It sure does, little man," Tim replied."

"Who are they?" asked Peggy.

"It's a group from the adventure playground in the city. Their schools have already broken up, so

we've got an early booking. They sound alright."
Peggy laughed. "Let's hope so – not like the last lot
who nearly set fire to the woods."

After breakfast on Saturday morning, they walked
the short distance along the towpath to where Odin
and Thor were moored. Tim pushed a wheelbarrow
loaded with a large can of engine oil, two jerry cans
full of red diesel fuel and a sack of coal. Peggy and
Zed carried plastic buckets full of cleaning materials
and toilet rolls. Sammy and Sheena, Tim's two
adopted swans, swam alongside. Peggy waved to
Jean Lovell, who was opening the canal shop.

Tim unloaded the contents of the wheelbarrow
onto the towpath. Peggy and Zed went to the bow of
Odin and unclipped the canvas. Peggy asked Zed to
undo all the clips so she could roll the canvas up
along the full length of the boat. Tim put a big yellow
funnel into the filling hole at the top of the fuel tank
on Odin. Lifting up one of the cans, he poured in the
diesel. The cover was rolled up and clipped onto the
walk board on the top. Peggy and Zed went inside.
Peggy filled a big pot with water and put it on the
stove to heat up. Zed had been asked to take all of the
mattresses off the bunks so they could be wiped
down. Tim checked the oil and water levels in the
engine. Peggy opened the cupboards to check that
the right number of plates and dishes, pots and pans
were in the galley. Tim uncoiled the hosepipe and

connected it to the tap on the side of the towpath. He put the other end into the nozzle on top of the water tank and turned on the tap. He knew it was empty and would take a long time to fill. Peggy tipped the hot water into two buckets and added some floor cleaner. She and Zed mopped the boat through. Tim went to the bow locker to check the gas bottles were full so that the cooking stoves would work. They were, so he closed the hatch.

Tim crossed to Thor, the butty. This didn't have an engine. He unlocked the doors to the little cabin at the stern and took out the long wooden tiller bar. He connected it to the boat. When Peggy and Zed had finished cleaning Odin, they, too, crossed over to Thor. Barney had long since got bored and run up to the canal shop in the hope of a biscuit from Jean. The morning passed quickly. Peggy made some tea and they sat on the grass next to the boats. Tim sent Zed up to the canal shop for a loaf so he could feed Sammy and Sheena. Barney returned with Zed and stood barking at the two swans. They took no notice. If ever they got too close or flapped their wings, Barney ran away. He was all bark!

Saturday was changeover day at Harry Martin's small boat hire company. Although he had 12 boats, it was a small fleet compared to some of the big hire companies on the canal, who had over 30. From early Saturday morning, hirers would be returning their boats to the boatyard. A group of local ladies would arrive to clean the boats and change the bedding. Harry's two boatmen would check the engines on all of the boats that had come back in. They would then refill the fuel and pump out the toilets. At 3 o'clock, the new hirers would arrive to take over their boats. Often, if Harry was short staffed, Tim and Peggy would help with the turnaround.

Some of the hirers were very experienced and had been using Harry's boats for years. Others were new to boating on the canals and time would be spent showing them how to handle the boats and work the locks. Harry got very annoyed when he heard that some hire companies sent out boats without giving the hirers proper instruction – he said it was dangerous and irresponsible and could lead to accidents.

It was the middle of the afternoon when they finished the work on Odin and Thor. When they arrived back at the cottage, the first of Harry's boats was coming into the lock. Peggy and Zed stood at the top gate looking down into the chamber as the boat came in. Peggy would know very quickly if they were experienced or not. They weren't. Peggy smiled at the young man and woman in their early twenties who were walking along the side of the lock with the windlasses.

"You OK, love?" she asked the woman. The woman explained that they had never been on a boat before and were a bit worried about operating their first lock, even though they had been shown what to do at the boatyard.

"No worries, dear," said Peggy, "we all have to start somewhere. Would you like us to give you a hand?"

They were very pleased with this offer and watched carefully as Peggy and Zed showed them how to work the boat through the lock. Slowly the boat rose uphill as the water fell in from the canal above. The man steering was their brother. He told Peggy that they hadn't been away on holiday together since they were teenagers, so had decided to do something different this summer. Their black Labrador, Roy, had jumped off and was making friends with Barney. When the water in the chamber was level with the canal, Zed pushed open the gates.

"Have a good trip," called Peggy as they steered out of the lock.

They waved goodbye. By seven o'clock that evening, eight hire boats had passed through the lock. Four of them were newcomers and were grateful for the help that Peggy and Zed gave them.

Tim had walked across the meadow to the village. He always met up with some friends in the Red Lion pub on a Saturday afternoon. He would have two pints of beer and a game of darts, catch up with the gossip on the canal and walk back to his cottage. Barney would normally go with him but wanted to stay with Zed instead. Tim had called him a turncoat before he left.

When Tim returned from the village, they sat down to a dinner of sausages and mash with fried onions, followed by fruit salad and ice cream. Zed was tired. It had been a long day and he had worked hard that morning.

CHAPTER SEVEN:

The Youth Group

They were all up early on Sunday morning. The youth group from the adventure playground would arrive at nine o'clock. Tim put their bags and sleeping bags into the wheelbarrow and took them to where the boats were moored. It had been agreed that they would eat with the group, so Peggy didn't have to worry about buying any food, apart from Barney's meat and biscuits. When Tim had returned from the boats, they ate a quick breakfast of toast and cornflakes and waited for the youth group to arrive.

Barney heard the noise first and ran barking down the track towards the lane to the village. Very soon, a blue mini bus appeared. It had a roof rack loaded with luggage, and a trailer. The mini bus pulled up next to the cottage and three young adults jumped out.

"Hi, I'm Matt," said one of them shaking Tim's hand, "and this is Paula and Rik. We're the youth workers with the group. You must be Tim."

"I am indeed, and this is Peggy and Zed, welcome."

"Hey, this is cool." said Matt looking across at the double lock. "Certainly beats our area – all traffic and concrete."

"Have any of you been on a narrow boat trip before?" asked Tim.

"Never," replied Paula, "we're definitely looking forward to it."

"Good stuff." said Peggy, "and it looks like fine weather too."

"Come on you, lot," shouted Matt, banging on the side of the mini bus, "wakey, wakey!"

In no time at all, Tim was surrounded by a large group of youngsters with an assortment of fishing rods, rucksacks, cases, and even two large bulging launderette bags, with enough food for an army.

"This is Tim and Peggy," said Matt. "They're going to be our skippers for the weekend, and this is Zed." Tim and Peggy both smiled at the excited children, although some of them looked a little sleepy after their journey.

"OK", said Tim, "shall we walk along to where the boats are?"

They walked the short distance along the towpath to where the two 70 foot canvas topped boats "Odin" and "Thor" were moored. Both boats were made of steel, but only Odin had an engine. "Thor" was a butty and was moved along the canal by being tied by a rope to "Odin" and pulled along behind. On wide stretches of the canal, they would travel alongside each other. Tim had been using the boats for over 30 years, and they were the only boats of their kind still going. Each had 12 bunk beds, toilets (which Tim called "bucket-and-chuck-its"), a galley kitchen with folding tables and benches, and a wonderful wood-burning stove. At the back of each boat, there were small skipper's cabins – one for Tim, and the other for Peggy, where they stayed when they were on board. Tim's cabin looked just like the one his grandparents used to have on their boat. They were known as "boat people" and had lived on board a pair of narrow boats carrying coal along the Grand Union Canal. Tim could just remember being taken on board their boats when he was very young, and could still recall the cosy and warm cabins they lived in. He also remembered how everything on the boat seemed to be painted in brilliant colours – red, green, blue and yellow. Tim and Peggy often took groups of youngsters and community groups from the towns and cities away on trips on the boats for weekends, or sometimes longer. It had already been decided that the boys would go onto Thor, the butty, and the girls on Odin.

Tim opened the front doors and side hatches to both boats. He took the youth workers on board first to show them the layout inside and explain where everything was kept.

"I suggest you organise your gear down below first, then you follow it," he said. "See you shortly."

He disappeared onto Odin to do the engine checks. Even after all these years, he still used the method his father had taught him to remember everything. His dad had made sure that Tim knew how important it was to make sure that everything on the boat was working properly and safely before leaving. Peggy and Zed went to the stern cabin of Thor to check on the spare ropes and first aid kit.

Tim could hear the buzz of excited conversation from the group.

"Where's the shower?"

"Have you seen the toilet, it's a metal bin with a seat."

"Where do I plug my hairdryer in?"

"I'm not sleeping underneath you."

Tim smiled. He had heard it all before. Raised voices from the youth workers and the clatter of equipment being moved around were familiar sounds to him.

They had agreed to all meet back on the towpath at 10 o'clock, so Tim could talk to them about safety and explain how important it was to be careful about using fresh water and electricity, and for him or Peggy to answer any questions the children might have.

They didn't have to wait long for the first question.

"When can we go fishing?"

"This evening," said Tim, "After we moor up for the night."

"What kind of fish are in the canal?

"Roach, bream, carp and perch, replied Tim," and if you're very unlucky, you might catch a pike."

"Can we go swimming?"

"No, we do not swim in the canal. It can make you really sick."

"What happens if someone falls in?"

"Or is pushed in," someone shouted.

They all laughed loudly.

"Are there any snakes on the bank?"

Peggy answered. "Oh yes, huge ones, aren't there, Tim?"

"Some are about 9 or 10 metres long," said Tim. They wait in the trees for you to pass by, and then drop on to you."

For a few seconds, there was a look of surprise and fright on the faces of some of the youngsters, including Zed.

"We're only kidding," Peggy said, laughing loudly. "There's no such thing."

Someone else was about to ask something when Matt interrupted. "Hey, you lot, hang on or we'll be here all day with these questions."

"Before we go anywhere, we need to get everyone fitted with a buoyancy aid," said Tim. Peggy and Zed went inside Odin and came out with lots of red and blue buoyancy aids. They were all numbered. Tim called Zed forward so he could use him to demonstrate how to wear one. Zed pulled up the zip and fastened the buckle at the front. He told the group that they should always be done up tightly.

"You always wear your buoyancy aid when you are up top or working the locks," he said.

Peggy gave out one to each member of the group and asked them to remember the number. She explained that it was their responsibility to look after it. When everyone had been issued with one each, Tim asked them all to put them on. Tim and Peggy then walked along the group, making sure they were all fastened tightly.

The group split into their boat crews and went aboard Odin and Thor. Tim called the youth workers together and explained how to cast off from the towpath.

Peggy, Zed and some of the youngsters had pulled Thor behind Odin ready to be towed. It was agreed that Matt would manage the bowline at the front of the boat, and Paula would unfasten the stern line at the back of the boat. Peggy and Zed were now on the stern of Thor, with Peggy holding the large wooden tiller bar, which was used to steer the boat. Tim was on the stern end of Odin, with Barney beside him.

"Right, let go," he shouted loudly. Matt and Paula untied the lines, gave a shove and jumped on. Odin moved slowly away from the bank, and then with a jolt, Thor followed, being pulled along by the towrope which was tied to Odin. The canvas roof of the boats had already been rolled back and some of the youngsters were actually sunbathing on their bunks. The others were sitting at the front of the boat, watching the water as it flowed past.

As they approached the first lock, Tim and Peggy pulled Thor alongside Odin.

"It's clever how you do that," said Matt, "very smooth."

Tim and Peggy steered the boats towards the canal bank and Matt and Paula jumped off holding the ropes, or "lines" as Tim called them.

"OK, tie the lines off," called Tim.

When the boats were safely tied up, everyone walked up to the first lock so Tim and Peggy could explain how the lock worked, and what they needed to do to help the boats go through. Peggy told them that a lock was like a staircase – a way of getting a boat up and over hills. They were very careful to show the group how to use the windlass and explained all the different parts of the lock. "Right," said Tim, "from now on, we'll be in two groups and take it in turns to work the locks.

It was early afternoon and getting very warm. All of the group had now changed into shorts and were sunbathing on their bunks. Zed was sitting on the stern with Tim. Barney had moved into Tim's cabin in search of some shade and Peggy was steering Thor, wearing her wide-brimmed straw hat.

"We'll soon be arriving at the tunnel," said Tim.

"Is it very long?" asked Zed.

"Yes," replied Tim "over a mile, and very dark and cool."

They moored the boats outside the tunnel entrance. As Tim and Peggy moved Thor behind Odin, the group of children lay out of the sun under a huge tree.

"How old is the tunnel?" asked Rik as Tim jumped from Odin onto the towpath.

"It was built in 1796," said Tim, "and quite a few of the navvies were either killed or injured when it was built."

"What's a navvie?" asked Rik.

"The word navvie is short for a navigator," replied Tim, "and they were really tough men who were very good at digging, and moving earth and rocks by hand. Not many of them lived past 40 though, and don't forget that the main tool they had was a shovel."

"That's unbelievable," said Rik, looking into the mouth of the tunnel and then walking over to explain it to the group.

Tim and Peggy joined them under the large tree, and Matt handed them both mugs of tea, as Rik and Paula handed out sausage rolls, crisps and cold drinks to the group.

"Hey Peggy!" someone called out. She looked up to see two boys sitting on the branch of the tree.

"You know you told us they used to pull the boats by horses?"

"Yes," Peggy replied.

"Well, how did the boats get through the tunnel without the horse pulling them?"

"The boat had to be legged through the tunnels, and the horse would be taken over the hill to meet the boat on the other side."

"Legged, what does that mean?" the boy asked.

"Come down from the tree, and I'll show you."

Peggy walked to the moored boats, followed by nearly all the group. She took the plank of wood from the top of Odin and slid it under the guy straps of the canvas cover at the bow of the boat.

"OK," she said, "imagine now that the boat is in the tunnel and one person would lie on their back on the plank of wood, with their legs over the side of the boat and their feet on the wall of the tunnel. The same thing would happen on the other side of the boat with another person. Lying flat like that, they would push their feet against the tunnel wall and do a sideways walk that would pull the boat along with them. So think yourself lucky we have an engine."

She also told them that when the canals were being built, it would take a gang of 100 men three weeks to dig out a mile stretch with a pickaxe, shovel and wheelbarrow.

As the boat entered the tunnel, the cool air provided relief from the heat outside. The youngsters wanted to shout and whistle to hear the echo, but Tim had asked them not to, in case someone accidentally fell into the water and couldn't be heard shouting for help. Two large headlights on the boat lit up the streams of water falling from the ventilation shafts built into the roof that were there to let air in and out of the tunnel. When they looked back at the tunnel entrance, it had shrunk to a small marble of light behind them. They moved slowly through the tunnel, occasionally bumping into the uneven walls, and it soon became completely dark, as they could see no daylight behind or in front of them. A little while later and a bit further on, they saw a tiny glare of sunlight slowly grow in size as they came to the end of the tunnel. As they came out of the tunnel, the bright sun and hot air seemed to cover them like a cloud of heat and light, and for a moment, they couldn't see properly.

"Wow, it's hot out here," Peggy called to Tim. "Let's reverse back into the tunnel!"

"No way!" shouted Tim, "on we go."

It was late in the afternoon by the time Tim decided to moor for the night by Old Mill Lock, where the canal meets the river before it disappears under the viaduct carrying the railway track over the valley. Peggy told Zed that a long time ago, the mill used to make copper sheets for protecting the hulls of wooden warships, but was now a disused building. Tim had been watching the sky for some time now, and he had noticed large grey balls of cloud, slowly swallowing the blue sky that had been with them since morning.

A small iron bridge connected the towpath to the edge of the wood on the opposite side of the canal, where large willow trees overhung the water. Although there were several moorings on this side of the canal, there was only one boat moored up. This pleased Tim and Peggy, as it meant fewer people for the group to disturb.

Soon the youngsters had started to explore the area. They had slung a rope swing over a small stream that ran from the wood into the canal. Those that had brought fishing rods were setting them up along the bank. Peggy had already used the boat pole from the roof to rescue two footballs from the lock chamber. Tim was in the engine room, checking the stern gland on Odin and wiping the engine down with a rag.

Peggy and Zed had taken Barney for a walk in the woods. Peggy had tried to get Zed to play with the other youngsters but he preferred to stay with her and Barney. She had noticed, though, that he had made friends with one particular lad called Simon, who seemed to spend a lot of time on his own.

"Did you have any close friends when you lived in London?" Peggy asked.

"Not really. Gran didn't like me mixing with the other kids on the estate. She thought I'd get into trouble."

"What do you think of this group?"

"Alright," he said, "Bit noisy though. I like that Simon. 'E's nice and likes fishing and things."

He told Peggy that Simon had come from a place called Ghana and had only lived here for two years.

"Didn't you have any friends at the circus?" asked Peggy.

"No, all the kids was a lot older than me."

Barney had disappeared into the long undergrowth.

"He can smell the foxes", said Peggy. "Come on, Barney" she called, "we're going back now."

Matt waved to the woman standing next to the small narrow boat moored underneath the willow trees on the other side of the canal.

"Hope they're not disturbing you."

"Not at all," she said, "good to see them enjoying themselves."

Jenny and Whisky, her black and white cocker spaniel, had lived aboard her boat, Ruskin, for two years. After her husband had died she found herself staring at the four walls of her house and decided that she needed do something very different, so she had sold the house and moved onto a boat. Jenny and her husband used to hire a boat for their summer holidays every year, so she had a good idea of what was involved in living aboard. Peggy had met Jenny before, when pumping the toilets out at Harry Martin's boatyard.

"Hello, my dear," called Peggy, waving to Jenny from the iron bridge. "It's been a lovely day."

"Too warm," replied Jenny, "I think we might have a storm tonight."

"Hope not," called Peggy, "we have a barbecue later."

"That sounds fun," said Jenny.

"Why don't you join us?"

Jenny was pleased to, it did get a little lonely sometimes with just her and Whisky.

"Thanks," she said, "I look forward to it."

Tim had set the barbecue up on the strip of grass between the towpath and the wall of the old mill. Matt and Paula were cooking piles of sausages and beef burgers on a mesh grill that rested on the top of an oil drum that had been cut in half. Tim always carried it on the boat with a good supply of logs and coal. Paula and Peggy were adding the cobs of sweet corn and beans to the plastic plates and passing them round to the group, who were sitting on a fallen tree. Zed, Simon and two other boys were sitting on the roof of Thor. Jenny was handing out cola in large plastic cups.

"Tim," shouted Matt, "you ready to eat?"

"Won't be long," Tim called back from the stern of Odin.

After they had all finished eating and the clearing up was done, Matt sat down with his guitar and he and Paula organised a sing-song for the group. Tim, Peggy, Jenny and Rik sat in fold-up chairs on the grass. It was still very warm. Peggy was surprised how many of the youngsters joined in with the singing. Rik finished off the evening with a ghost story. It was all about "Black Jack," who used to haunt the mill locks.

Rik told the hushed group how "Black Jack" used to hold up the working boats and rob them as they went through the lock. When he was eventually caught, a group of angry boatmen hung him from the tree next to the lock. After the story, Rik took them to the lock and showed them the tree.

Walking back to the fire, they all stayed very close together.

The grey clouds had turned black and Tim thought he saw a flash of lightning in the distance. Peggy said it wasn't lightning but from a passing train. Barney and Whisky were fast asleep, their own dinner untouched, as they had been fed more than enough beef burgers and sausages by the youngsters.

Soon, distant flashes of lightning and low rumbles of thunder seemed to surround them on all sides. "I think we should get this lot onto the boats before the heavens open," said Matt.

The wind had picked up and Tim decided to soak the barbecue fire.

"We don't want any of these hot embers falling on that dry grass," he said, pouring a large bucket of canal water over the top.

"Come on, Whisky," said Jenny, "time to go home before we get wet, too. Thanks for a good evening, all."

"Any time," replied Peggy, "see you in the morning. Sleep well."

Inside Odin and Thor, plastic bowls had been laid out on the trestle tables so the youngsters could wash and clean their teeth before they went to bed. A large pot of hot chocolate was on the stove, and sleeping bags were being laid out. Tim and Peggy had gone to their cabins at the stern of each boat. Zed was sleeping on Thor, on the bunk bed above Simon. None of the group except Zed had slept on a boat before and soon the gentle rocking and tiredness of a long day sent them into a deep sleep. The youth workers were surprised – normally the first night away was madness and they would be awake all night. The lights went out on both boats at 11 o'clock and soon all that could be heard was the distant rumbling of thunder and occasional snoring.

In the early hours of the morning, a lightning flash lit up the boats like the coming of daylight, followed by an enormous crash of thunder. The rain fell like a waterfall pounding on the canvas roof of the boats, followed by another bright flash and another roar of thunder. Everyone was now awake. Tim pulled on his waterproofs and boots, grabbed his torch and pushed open the doors of his cabin. Barney jumped onto Tim's bed and burrowed under the duvet. The pellets of rain bit into Tim's face as he made his way along the towpath to the bow of the boat. Unzipping the canvas, he climbed down the steps.

"Everybody OK?" he asked, the water running from his oilskin coat onto the floor. "No leaks?"

"Only you," said Paula, laughing.

All the girls were now sitting up in their sleeping bags.

"You lot all right?" shouted Tim.

Apart from one little girl who thought the canvas might give way, they seemed fine. Peggy was up on Thor and checking on the boys.

Tim was about to go back to his cabin when they heard a loud crash

"Blimey," said Paula, "what was that?"

"Sounds like a tree's come down," said Tim, "I'll have a look."

Standing on the towpath, he shone his powerful torch all around him. The rain was still falling heavily and it was very dark, making it difficult to see. Then he saw it: a large willow tree had fallen across Jenny's boat, completely covering it. He could see the light was on inside. Running across the bridge, he made his way along the slippery towpath towards Jenny's boat.

The thick trunk of the tree had fallen across the bow end completely blocking the doors. Being a small boat there were no doors at the stern end, so the only way out was through the front doors. "Jenny," called Tim, "Are you alright?"

"Bit shaken," he heard her say, "I've cut my head bad. Whisky is very frightened, and I can't open the doors."

"Hang on," called Tim, "I'll get some help."

Crossing back over the bridge, he met Peggy at the bottom of the steps.

"Quick, get the others," he said, "a tree's fallen on Jenny's boat – she can't get out."

Matt and Rik ran to the bridge with Peggy while Paula stayed with the youngsters on the boats. They jumped onto the bow end of Jenny's boat and tried pulling and pushing the tree, but it was too heavy and wouldn't move.

"What about the axe, Tim?" said Peggy,

"No – it'll take too long to cut through this. We will have to pull it off somehow."

111

"How about the kids?" said Matt. "They could help."

Tim thought for a moment.

"There's not enough room around this side for them all to stand, but we could still use them."

Tim asked Matt to go with Peggy and fetch all of the long ropes from the boats. He also asked them to bring the first aid kit back with them. Rik ran back to the boats to organize the youngsters.

They were still wide awake and sitting up in their bunks when Rik came back on board.

"We need your help," he said, and quickly explained what had happened to Jenny.

They jumped from their bunks, keen to make the most of the adventure. Some got dressed. Most just pulled their waterproofs on over their nightwear. They all gathered together on the towpath. The rain had eased and the air was still warm, but it was the dark that surprised the youngsters the most. They had never seen such blackness. Along the towpath, they saw two bright lights appear. Peggy had lit some hurricane lamps and put them on a wooden seat.

"Come on, you lot," she called, "over here." They all moved quickly to where Peggy was standing.

Tim had joined all the ropes together with sheet bend knots. This was a special knot for tying ropes of unequal thickness together. He tied another knot called a timber hitch around the trunk of the tree that was across Jenny's boat. He had then taken the other end of the rope over the bridge to where the group were now standing.

"Right," shouted Tim, "I want you all to take hold of the rope and get into a straight line, just like a tug of war."

Barney had joined them and was keen to be involved. He took the end of the rope in his teeth and started pulling.

"Not yet, you silly dog," shouted Tim.

"Ready, everybody? Now get a good grip on the ground, and when I shout 'go,' I want you all to pull on the rope as hard as you can. OK – take the strain."

The rope tightened and lifted up from the water.

Tim shouted as loud as he could. "Go, go!"

A few youngsters lost their footing on the slippery ground and fell down.

"Is it moving?" called Peggy.

"A bit," Tim replied. "OK, everyone, take a break."

There was a loud splash as the rope dropped back into the water.

"Right," called Tim, "everything you've got this time. Ready – take the strain and pull, pull."

They all strained and dug their feet into the ground. Suddenly, with a loud crash, the tree fell from the roof into the canal. A huge cheer went up.

"Well done!" shouted Tim, "well done, everybody!"

Rik was trained in first aid and had run across the bridge with the first aid kit to help Jenny and dress the cut on her head. Tim and Peggy followed behind him.

"How did you do this?" asked Rik, putting a large plaster on Jenny's head.

"It was that big clap of thunder. I sat up with such a start that I hit my head on the edge of the bookshelf." Peggy made Jenny a cup of hot, sweet tea and said she would keep her company for the rest of the night.

Back on board the camper boats, the youngsters drank cups of hot chocolate and ate biscuits then climbed wearily back into their bunks. Their discarded clothes lay on the floor where they fell. Matt and Paula thanked them all for their help before falling exhausted into their own bunks.

When morning came there was not a sound from inside the boats. Everyone was fast asleep. The stormy weather had been replaced by a cool, gentle breeze. The canvas roof of the boats was covered in broken branches and leaves. A patchwork of muddy puddles covered the towpath. It was 10 o'clock before Matt crawled from his bunk in search of a much needed coffee. Midday had passed by the time they were all up and had their breakfast. Tim and Peggy had been up since 8 o'clock and had already turned the boats around in the winding hole, steered them past the fallen tree and back to the mooring. The group didn't even know that the boats had moved.

Matt and Paula called all the youngsters onto the

towpath where Jenny and Whisky were waiting with two large plastic carrier bags.

"Whisky and I would like to thank you all for your help last night, and these are for you," she said.

She had got up early and walked across some fields to the nearest village shop to buy sweets and chocolate. Jenny handed them to Paula to give out and then gave her a kiss on the cheek.

"That's for everyone," she said.

"Well," called Tim, "it's time we were away. Time and tide and all that stuff."

Peggy laughed. "What tide?"

Jenny and Whisky crossed the bridge over the canal to her boat. Whisky barked and wagged his tail. Barney replied, and then jumped onto the stern with Tim. As they entered Mill Lock, the gates crashed behind them. "Up paddles," shouted Tim, as their downhill homeward journey began.

As they had left Mill Lock in the afternoon, they needed to make good time on the way back. Otherwise, the group would be not be home until midnight. Tim was pleased by how well the youngsters were working together. One team was running ahead to get the next lock ready. They would open the top ground and gate paddles and fill the lock with water, so when the boats arrived, they could go straight in. The other team would work the boats through the lock by holding the lines and emptying the lock so the boats could go out through the bottom gates. Whenever he could, Tim kept the two boats alongside each other and only had to drop Thor behind on tow when the canal narrowed. Barney stayed close to Zed, who was in Paula's group. Simon was in the same group and Peggy noticed how he was eager to learn all the things that Zed knew. She was pleased that at last Zed had found a friend.

The warm breeze that blew that day was ideal for drying all of the wet clothes and waterproofs from the storm the night before. Peggy had rolled back the canvas roof on each boat and the youth workers had put a long washing line from one end to the other. Tim had laid the long ropes that they had used to pull the tree off Jenny's boat along the walk plank, so they could dry in the sun. Several people who were walking or cycling along the towpath laughed as this "floating laundry" went by.

It was early evening when they reached the mooring for Odin and Thor, which was just by the canal shop. They had eaten lunch on the move and everybody was very tired. All their bags had been packed and everything cleaned while they were on the move and as soon as the boats were tied up to the bank, they unloaded all the gear onto the towpath. Tim, Peggy, and Zed walked with them to Tim's cottage, where the mini bus was parked. Zed had got Simon's mobile number. He didn't have a phone, so he had given Simon Peggy's number. When all the bags had been packed into the trailer or loaded onto the roof rack of the mini bus, Matt called the youngsters together to say thanks and goodbye. Tim said they had been a great group and were welcome to come back any time. Paula said she would try to organise another trip for the October half term. They all said they would like to come again. Zed was sad to see Simon go. They had got on really well and Simon said he would ring Zed next week. Matt tooted the horn as they turned out of the track onto the lane and they were gone. Zed asked Peggy and Tim if Simon could come and stay during his school holidays. They both agreed it was a good idea and Peggy said she would speak to his parents when he rang.

Tim walked back to the boats to close them down properly while Peggy and Zed took their bags into the cottage. Peggy was in the kitchen putting the dirty clothes in the washing machine when she called Zed to see if he wanted some supper. There was no reply. He had fallen fast asleep on the sofa.

CHAPTER EIGHT:

Six Weeks' Holiday

Zed woke at six thirty the next morning. He was soaked with sweat. Rubbing his eyes, he lay very still, staring at the ceiling. He closed his eyes tightly before opening them again quickly. He was still here in the room. His posters of wild animals were on the wall, his clothes were on the yellow wooden chair next to his bed and the mirror was still cracked on the old chest of drawers. He had dreamed that he was back with Darren in the circus. As a punishment for not selling enough programmes, Darren had made him climb the long wire ladder all the way up to the top of the big top tent and then sit on one of the swings that the trapeze artists used in their act. The circus ring was so far below it looked like a bottle top. He was swinging to and fro, then he was falling and screaming and the ground was getting closer – he woke up just in time.

Climbing out of bed, he opened the windows and breathed in the fresh morning air. He could feel the sweat drying on his body. Putting on his tracksuit, he crept through the sitting room and out of the front door. Sammy and Sheena were asleep on the grass, their long, thick necks tucked deep inside their white feathers. He sat on the balance beam for a long time, looking down into the empty lock chamber. Every so often, he would quickly close his eyes, then open them again. He was still here next to the canal with Tim and Peggy and Barney and it was for six weeks. It had all been a horrible dream.

He didn't hear Tim walk up behind him.

"Morning, Zed. Couldn't you sleep?"

Zed told Tim about the dream and how he was falling towards the circus ring. Tim sat on the balance beam next to him and told him to forget all about the circus, as he was never going back there.

Later, when Zed was in his room dressing, he found a large scrapbook with coloured pages in the drawer next to his bed. As it was empty, he decided to keep a log of all that happened during the six weeks. He remembered that at his last school, the teacher had asked all the children to talk about their holidays. He hadn't been on holiday, apart from a day trip to the coast organised by a church youth club on the estate, so he didn't have anything to talk about. Now, when he started at his new school in London in September, he could show them all his book and talk about the adventures he had with Tim and Peggy and Barney on the canals.

He wrote his name on the front cover. When he showed Peggy and told her what he was going to do, she wrote, "Stowaway" in big letters next to his name and gave him a pack of coloured pens and pencils and a little pot of glue. Tim gave him a photograph of Odin and Thor and another of Barney from when he first got him from the rescue centre.

Gran visited twice during the six weeks' holiday. She would stay with Peggy in her flat in the village and Zed would stay with Tim and Barney in the cottage. Gran was so pleased to see Zed enjoying himself and happy and looking so well.

Jean Lovell gave Zed a large postcard from the canal shop. It had a picture of the lock and Tim's white cottage on it. He addressed it to his mum in Holloway Prison, London and asked Gran to deliver it when she next visited her. In his scrapbook, he drew a picture as he remembered her with long red hair and a pale skin. Next to it, he put a window with bars and wrote above, in big letters, "Prison." Underneath, he wrote the same message that he had put onto the postcard:

Dear Mum

You would really like it here with Tim and Peggy and Barney on the canals.

I've been helping with the boats and doing some fishing and lots of other things.

You wouldn't need to take that stuff you do to stay happy 'cos it's so nice here and there are lots of fields and animals.

Wish you were here.

Love Zed xx

After their third fishing trip together, Tim had given Zed his own rod and keep net, with a little plastic box with pull-out trays that had hooks and floats in it. Zed found a shady place to fish between the lock and Harry Martin's boat yard. He would go there every day. He liked it because the towpath was wider here and there was a small patch of grass where he could pitch his tent. Not that he had one yet, but he imagined how wonderful it would be to camp overnight with Simon. He got to know a lot of the passing boaters and they would all wave and ask him what he had caught. When Tim had time, he would walk along the towpath and join him. Sometimes Peggy would go as well and sit reading a book.

One evening after dinner, Peggy's phone rang. It was Simon. She handed it to Zed and they spent a long time telling each other what they had been doing since they last saw each other. Zed told him about the fishing and the small grassed area where you could put a tent up. He asked Simon if he had ever been camping. He hadn't but said it sounded cool and would like to try it. Zed asked if he would like to come and stay. He said he would but would need to ask his dad. Zed also needed to ask Peggy and Tim. He would ring Simon again in the morning.

He thought it best to wait until Peggy's soaps had finished at nine o'clock before he asked about Simon coming to stay. Tim was sitting outside the cottage reading a book. Peggy turned off the television and went outside to join him. Zed followed.

"Peggy, Tim, you know Simon phoned earlier."

"Yes, dear," said Peggy.

"Well, I was wondering. Could he come and stay for a few days, we could do some fishing and…."

"And what?" asked Tim.

"Camping," Zed replied. "You know where I go fishing – we could camp there."

Peggy looked at Tim.

"Of course he can come to stay, love, but you don't have a tent, so how can you camp?"

Zed thought for a moment.

"We could make one," he said.

Tim smiled. "Good idea. Tell you what – you show me tomorrow how you'll make a tent and we'll see."

"Can I use some of the old plastic covers?" asked Zed.

"You can, and I'm sure you'll find something you can use for poles."

Peggy said she would speak to Simon's dad in the morning.

"Thanks Tim, Thanks Peggy."

Barney was looking at Zed with his head to one side.

"Yeah, you can come too," said Zed.

Before Zed went to sleep that night, he used a whole page of his scrapbook to draw a picture of the tent he would make the next day and the small grassed area by the canal where he and his new friend would pitch it. Then he drew the two of them sitting outside the tent, fishing by a big fire that they had lit. At the bottom of the page, he listed all the fish he had caught so far and on which day.

He was up early the next day and after quickly eating some breakfast, he went to the yard behind Tim's workshop. Peggy had gone into the village to do some shopping and Tim had taken his Land Rover into town to have a new tyre fitted. He knew there would be lots of bits here to build a tent from as Tim used it to store all sorts of equipment that he wasn't using. He found an old plastic sheet, and then looked around for some wood to make a frame to hold the sheet in place. He found some wooden poles and a roll of strong blue twine. It was nearly midday when he finished. He had put bricks around the edge of the plastic to keep it in place.

Zed heard Tim's Land Rover coming up the track. He ran to the cottage so he could show Tim the tent he had made.

"I've done it," he said to Tim. "I've made the tent."

"Well, well," replied Tim, "let's go and see it."

"There," said Zed, pointing to the blue plastic sheet held down by bricks.

Tim couldn't help smiling. "Very good, Zed, is it waterproof?"

"Course," said Zed.

"OK, jump inside and we'll test it."

Tim took the hosepipe off the back wall of the workshop as Zed crawled inside.

"Ready?" called Tim.

"Ready," said Zed.

Tim turned on the hose full pressure and squirted it at the tent. Soon the frame started to sway and then, with a crash, it fell down.

"I'm all wet!" Zed shouted, "turn it off!"

Tim was laughing loudly as a very wet Zed came

out from under the heap of plastic.

"That's not fair; you wouldn't get rain that 'ard."

Tim was still laughing when Peggy came into the yard.

"Good lord! What are you two up to?"

"I don't think his tent was too weatherproof," said Tim.

"Well," Peggy said, "it's just as well that we got this for you then Zed. She held out a long, round green bag.

"A tent!" shouted Zed. "Is it a tent?"

"It is," said Tim, "a real two man tent that will stand up in all weathers."

"Can I put it up now?"

"Come on love, we'll do it together," said Peggy.

"Watch out for sudden storms," called Tim. Zed laughed.

That night, Zed slept in his new tent on the grass outside the cottage. Barney kept him company. Tim gave him a big torch and left the front door of the cottage unlocked in case he decided to come indoors in the middle of the night. He drew a picture of his new tent in his scrapbook before turning off the torch and snuggling up to Barney.

Simon came to stay the following weekend. His dad dropped him off on Friday evening and said he would collect him on Monday afternoon. Their adventure would begin on Saturday morning, when they pitched their tent on the grassed area beside the towpath. Tim had lent Simon one of his fishing rods and Peggy had given them some food for dinner and breakfast to cook on the small gas stove. Simon caught the first fish. Zed said it was beginner's luck. Zed caught the next one, though it was smaller than Simon's. They stopped fishing early in the afternoon as it was getting too warm, and lay on the grass under the shade of a tree. Soon they had both fallen fast asleep. That evening, they cooked sausages and beans on their stove. Tim and Peggy wandered down the towpath to join them and they showed them the fish they had in the keep net.

It was a two-person tent, not a two boys and a dog tent. Barney was determined to be comfortable, which meant that the boys weren't. They both lay talking for a long time, occasionally turning the torch on when they heard a noise outside.

The dawn crept slowly into the tent. It took a few seconds for the boys to remember where they were. Barney was pawing the zip. He needed a bush urgently. When they looked out of the tent, all of the contents of their bag of food were spread along the towpath. Peggy had warned them not to leave it outside or the foxes would rummage through it, but in the dark they had forgotten. They finished off the chocolate and cola that Peggy had given them the night before.

They fished until midday. The final total of fish caught was Zed nine and Simon seven, although he said his were bigger than Zed's. They took the tent down and cleared everything up around them. Zed remembered what Tim had told him, that the only thing you leave in the countryside is your thanks.

That evening, after a hot shower, they sat down to a wonderful roast dinner that Peggy had cooked. They were both very hungry and after two helpings of everything, fell asleep.

The next day, Tim took them for a trip on a narrow boat called Tarn whose engine he had been servicing. He wanted to test that it was running properly. Tim steered while Zed and Simon worked the boat through the lock. Zed steered after the lock and they passed the place where they had camped the night before. Simon sat on the roof next to him. Tim had the cover to the engine off and was listening to the sound as the boat went along. They turned round in the entrance to Harry Martin's boatyard and headed back to the cottage. This was the first time that Zed had turned a boat around, with Tim showing him how to use the throttle and tiller to make the bow of the boat swing.

Simon's dad came at four o'clock in the afternoon. Simon said he would like to come again and that maybe Zed could come and stay with him in the city. Zed was sad to see him go and told Peggy he wished he had more friends like him. Peggy said she was sure that he would make some new friends when he started school in September.

In bed that night, Zed filled two pages of his scrapbook with drawings of his camping trip with him and Simon. He drew the ducks eating the bread that the foxes had spread along the towpath and a picture of him and Simon jumping into the canal in their boxer shorts and T-shirts for a swim. They had tried to get Barney in the water but he just stood on the bank and barked at them. They hadn't told Tim and Peggy about this, although Peggy had guessed when she emptied out their wet clothes. At the bottom of the page, he wrote Simon's address and mobile number and glued in a passport photograph that he had given him.

There were two more weekend boat trips on Odin and Thor. One was with a youth club from Swindon. They were very noisy and Tim said the youth workers weren't very good at keeping them under control. The other was a group of adults who wanted to keep mooring up all the time to take pictures of birds. They were nice people, though, and at the end of the trip, gave Zed a pair of binoculars. Zed had thought they must be something to do with the Queen as the name of their organisation started with the word "Royal" and they told him that she owned all of the swans in the country and they sometimes helped to number them. Zed didn't fancy trying to catch a swan, let alone put a number on it. He'd seen how Sammy and Sheena flapped their wings when Barney got too close to them.

On the inside cover of his scrapbook, Zed had numbered all of the days of the six weeks that he was staying with Tim and Peggy. Today he had crossed through 35. Only seven days to go until he went back to London. He didn't want to think about it. Gran had phoned last week and told Peggy that with Mrs. Phillips's help, they had got Zed into a secondary school near Surrey Quays. He knew he had to go back to school but was worried in case he didn't fit in with the other kids. Tim and Peggy had told him that he could come back and stay with them if he behaved and did well. Peggy had told Zed that Mrs. Phillips had offered to take him back to London by train on the Saturday. This would save his Gran from coming to collect him.

Tim often said that "time and tide wait for no man or boy" – usually when Zed was up late in the morning. Now, Zed's tide was ebbing away faster than he would have liked. Peggy had told him that the last few days of a holiday go quicker than the rest and she was right. He spent Thursday with Jean Lovell and Peggy at the canal shop. Jean had asked if he wanted to earn some pocket money by mowing the grass at the back of the shop. But Jack the goose had other ideas and kept attacking the lawn mower as Zed tried to keep it in a straight line. Zed had got to know Jack well and knew his weakness – popcorn. So every time he charged at the mower, Zed would throw some popcorn in the opposite direction.

Eventually, he was able to finish mowing the grass and Jean gave him five pounds.

It rained on Friday. He was glad and hoped that it would rain on Saturday. It would be easier to leave if it wasn't warm and sunny. Peggy had said that he had to visit everybody this morning to say goodbye, as Mrs. Phillips would be coming at nine o'clock on Saturday morning to collect him.

He walked along the towpath towards Harry Martin's boatyard. The grass was still flattened where he and Simon had camped. He passed the field where the little donkey always came to the gate for a carrot when people went by. Army Jim was sitting outside his green and brown camouflaged boat. His shirt and trousers were the same colour as his boat and he had a huge knife strapped to his leg. Zed said hello and hurried by. Tim said he was a bit odd but harmless. Zed wasn't so sure.

Harry was in his office, sitting in front of a computer.

"'Ello 'Arry," said Zed. "I've come to say goodbye."

Harry stood up. "So I hear, young Zed, so I hear." Harry always said everything twice. He opened a cupboard and took out a long box.

"This is for you, young Zed, to remember us by."

"What is it?" asked Zed.

"Well, open it and you'll find out, open it."

Inside was a wooden model of one of Harry's

boats. It was painted in his fleet colours of blue and red. Every detail was perfect. It even had two little rope fenders at the bow and stern. It was called "Stowaway."

"There, young man," said Harry. "Not many people can say they have had a boat named after them."

Zed didn't know what to say. Harry held out his hand for Zed to shake.

"You work hard at school, young Zed, you hear? Work hard and you can be anything you want. I'm sure we'll be seeing you again soon."

Walking back along the towpath, Zed called in to see Rocket Ron and his ferrets, Freddie and Frankie. He liked stroking them but was always afraid they might run up his trouser leg. He had told Zed about the time when Peggy's boat Turtle had caught fire and how he had got her out just in time. Zed knew that if it wasn't for Rocket Ron, he might never have met Peggy.

''Why do they call you Rocket Ron?'' asked Zed.

He Laughed. ''Well it's on account of me gas bottle that exploded one day and sent me flying over the hedge – just like a rocket''

''Wow'' said Zed, '' you could 'ave been killed''

''But I weren't, young Zed, I weren't, Lady Luck were looking after me that day''

"I'd better get going," said Zed, pulling Freddie from around his neck. Rocket Ron shook Zed's hand.

"Good luck, Zed – come back and see us soon."

Jean Lovell was sitting on the red bench outside the shop. Wills was next her and he was purring loudly. That meant he was happy. Zed was pleased, as Wills had very sharp claws and he could be so grumpy.

"Hello, Zed," said Jean, "off to London tomorrow, then?"

He sat down and showed her the model boat that Harry had given him.

"I have a present for you, too," she said. "You wait there."

She went inside the shop and came back with a framed picture of Odin and Thor that had been painted by a local artist.

Zed gave her a hug and said that he would always remember her and Wills and Jack.

"Listen to you," she said, "anyone would think we were never going to see you again."

That evening after dinner, Peggy watched her soaps on the television. Tim sat outside looking up at the tall beech tree. Zed lay on the grass by the lock with Barney, finishing off his scrapbook. He collected some mud from the canal bank in a tin tray and put Barney's paw in it, which he then pressed onto the page next to the picture of him.

That night, he took a long time to fall asleep. Both windows were open, as it was still warm outside. He could hear the water seepage running into the lock from the top gates and smell the freshly cut grass. This time tomorrow, he would be sleeping in his bed at Gran's flat in London and the smells and sounds would be very different from here. He was tired, but he didn't want to sleep. That would only make the morning come quicker. He remembered hearing an owl hoot from somewhere in the dark. Then it was light and Peggy was calling him. It was seven thirty in the morning.

Derek and Janice Phillips arrived at nine o'clock sharp. Derek would run them to the railway station in the town where they would catch the train to London Paddington.

"Well, Zed," said Tim, "Time to go, and we don't want any tears."

"No," said Peggy, "Or you'll start me off."

Zed hugged Tim, trying desperately not to cry.

"I only want to hear good things about you, young man," said Tim, patting him on the head.

Zed nodded. "You will, Tim, I promise."

Peggy looked at Zed. He had certainly changed in the six weeks he had been with them. He had put on weight and she was sure he had grown taller. The pale skin was now tanned and glowing. She pulled him towards her and gave him a big hug.

"You be a good boy at school and for your Gran."

He didn't want Tim to see the tears rolling down his cheeks, so he pushed his face hard into Peggy's T-shirt. Barney was sitting on the grass between the front door of the cottage and where the car was parked. Zed picked up his ball and threw it as hard as he could towards the lock. Barney ran after it. He always did. When he came back, Zed had gone. He was sitting in the back seat of the car. He couldn't bear to say goodbye to Barney. Tim and Peggy waved as the car drove away down the track. Barney lay with the ball between his front paws, looking confused. The next day Peggy would move back to her small flat over the butcher's shop in the village.

CHAPTER NINE:

London and School

On Sunday afternoon Zed stood on the balcony in front of his gran's flat on the eighth floor of Nelson House. All he could hear from far below was the noise of the traffic as it swept towards the large roundabout, before disappearing down the Rotherhithe Tunnel and under the River Thames, or towards Tower Bridge and the City of London. It was always busy, even on a Sunday. No longer could he hear the soothing babble of flowing water as it seeped through the gap in the leaky lock gates, or breathe in the sweet smell of the lavender bush that grew outside the front door of Tim's cottage. All this had been replaced by smelly exhaust fumes and pollution that hung like a cloud in the warm air.

He watched as a plane flew overhead on the flight path into City Airport, and wondered which country it had come from. Gran had taken him to City Airport once on the Docklands Light Railway. Zed had sat at the front of the train and pretended to be the driver, as the DLR trains were driverless. They had had a drink and a sandwich in the refreshments bar next to the departures lounge at the airport, and had watched through a large glass window as the planes landed and took off. Zed had been fascinated by how steeply they came in before landing on the short runway. How he had wanted to go in a plane that day and fly away somewhere, anywhere. 'One day, you will,' Gran had said. But he hadn't believed her. Only rich people went in planes. He knew Gran and Mum had never been in one, so why should he be so lucky?

Zed's bedroom had been redecorated since he had last slept in it. Gran had bought him a new bed and wardrobe, and the carpet had been cleaned. He had put the model narrowboat that Harry Martin had given him on the shelf underneath the picture of Tim's boats 'Odin' and 'Thor', then pinned all of the postcards that he had collected around it. Above those he put a letter from his mum, thanking him for the postcard he had sent her in prison.

That evening Gran ordered his favourite Pepperoni pizza, with some garlic bread. The young guy delivering the pizza wasn't happy as the lift had broken down and he had had to walk all the way up the stairs, and he was worried about leaving his moped outside the flats in case it got stolen. Gran felt sorry for him and gave him a pound tip. After dinner Zed sat with Gran, looking through his scrapbook. She knew that the next few weeks would be very hard for him, as he had not been to school for a long time, and could well struggle to keep up.

Peggy rang on Sunday evening. She and Gran had a long chat about the latest episodes of the soaps before Zed was able to ask her about Tim and Barney. She said Barney was missing him already and kept going into his bedroom to look for him, and of course Tim missed him but he would never admit it. He told Peggy that he had gone shopping with Gran to Surrey Quays in the morning to get some stuff for school. Peggy asked about his uniform. He said it was just a green polo shirt and sweatshirt with grey trousers. She wished him luck at his new school and told him to behave himself.

'Can I come and stay with you again at Easter?' he asked.

'Well, that's up to Gran,' she said, 'but provided you are a good boy and do well at school I don't see why not.'

'I will be good Peggy, you'll see, 'bye then.' He handed the phone back to Gran.

Zed was lying on the sofa watching the television, and flicking from one channel to another, whilst drinking from a large carton of cola that had come with the pizza. He heard the phone ring, and a few minutes later his Gran called out to him.

'Zed, love, your mum's on the phone.'

He raced into the kitchen and grabbed the phone from Gran's hand.

Mum said she didn't have long, but wanted to wish him well in his new school, she also told him that they were moving her to an Open Prison which she was looking forward to. It was strange, Zed always wanted to tell her so much, but there was never enough time, so he told her a joke instead. 'How do you stop a dog barking in the back garden?' Mum didn't know. 'Put it in the front garden!' She laughed; it was good to hear her laugh.

Kevin Brady was a friend of Zed's and lived on the fourth floor of Trafalgar Block across the road with his mum and sister. Kevin had a one-eyed cat called Eric. He used to have both eyes until somebody shot him one day with an air gun. Kevin had found him lying bleeding by the rubbish bins and had taken him home. That had been three years ago, and after an operation at a local animal charity centre his mum had said he could keep him, and they had been inseparable ever since.

Kevin was starting at the same secondary school as Zed, and would be going with him on Monday morning. He had been in the same class as Zed at St Mary's Junior School, and was sitting next to Lee Young when Zed had thrown the chair at Lee, knocking out one of his teeth and cutting his head. Kevin had been warning Lee to stop taking the mickey out of Zed's mum and calling her a 'jailbird', but he had carried on taunting Zed. Although Kevin had tried to explain to the Head Teacher that Lee had very much asked for it when Zed had thrown the chair at him, Zed had still been excluded. Kevin's mum said it was because Lee Young's mother was a school governor.

When Zed woke on Monday morning after a sleepless night he felt sick, and longed to be back in the country with Tim, Peggy and Barney. He picked up the mobile phone that Gran had bought him as an early Christmas present. It was ten past six. The alarm was set to go off at seven o clock, so he curled up in the dark under the duvet, and wished time would stand still. But as Tim always said, 'time and tide wait for no man', and dead on the stroke of seven an annoying series of beeps from the mobile drove Zed out of bed, and into the shower, with some firm encouragement from Gran.

Zed changed into his new school uniform, and went through to the kitchen where Gran had put some breakfast cereal and toast on the table, but he couldn't face it. Kevin knocked for him at eight o'clock. He told Zed that Eric had followed him all the way down the stairs to the ground floor.

They left the flat and walked the short distance through the estate to the busy main road. Lots of children, all wearing green polo shirts and sweatshirts seemed to pour from every corner and then merge into one noisy group by the crossing. The old lollipop man in his yellow coat and hat didn't seem too friendly, and the older kids would take the mickey out of him, and then run across the road before he had a chance to stop the traffic. More cautious, Zed and Kevin waited for the lollipop man to step out before running across themselves.

There were two parts to the school, the main building and the annexe. They would be in the annexe with all the other Year Seven students. During the morning assembly, the Head of Year, Mr Day, welcomed them to the school before they were broken up into their different tutor groups. Zed and Kevin were in the same group and their tutor was a young female teacher called Miss Swan. She reminded Zed of Sammy and Sheena, not just because of her name but also because she had a long white neck.

After giving out their timetable of lessons for the week, Miss Swan said that as an ice breaker, so they could all get to know each other, she wanted them each to talk for five minutes on what they had done in the six-week school holiday. She asked that the next day they should all bring in to school something to support their talk such as postcards or photographs, and that there would be a prize for the winner.

After registration the next morning Miss Swan said that she would start first, and spoke about the two weeks she had spent with her partner in the Lake District, walking and climbing. She then showed them some pictures of her standing on top of a mountain called 'Scafell Pike' which was 978 meters high.

'Is that as high as Mount Everest, Miss?' called one girl.

Miss Swan laughed, 'No, Kate, Everest is much higher. I don't think we could have made it to the top of that.'

Many of the children had been away on day trips organised by local youth clubs and church groups, mainly to theme parks and the coast. A few children had been to a holiday camp with the family, and a lucky couple to Spain; one girl spoke of visiting her family in Nigeria.

When it came to Zed's turn, he told the class about how he had run away from the circus and stowed away on a narrow boat; how he had stayed for six weeks with Peggy and Tim on the canals, and about Barney, Tim's collie. He was just about to show them his scrapbook when Miss Swan stopped him.

"Sorry, Zed. Time's up. You do seem to have had a busy time."

He could see from her face and those of some of his classmates that they thought he was making it all up. When he sat down, even Kevin asked him if it was really true.

"What, you think I'm making all that up?"

He put his scrapbook onto Miss Swan's desk. There was an assortment of postcards and photographs. The girl who had been to Nigeria had brought in her plane tickets to a place called 'Lagos'. He noticed a brochure from a holiday camp and a programme from an activity centre in Kent. This reminded him of Dean Cherry, the canoe instructor who he had met with Tim. Miss Swan told the class that the winner would be announced at three o'clock, when they returned to their tutor group after their last lesson.

When they arrived back in the afternoon, Miss Swan was sitting on the edge of her desk looking at a piece of paper. She said that she had judged each person's talk and given extra points for the quality of material they had brought in and she was now going to announce the winner. There was a pause and the class went quiet.

"The winner of the ten pound book token is…….. Zed Hawkins."

They all clapped as Zed walked to the front of the class to receive his prize.

"You didn't believe me at first, did you Miss?" he said as he took the book token from her.

Zed had never won anything before, let alone a school prize, and walking home he was really excited about telling Gran.

'What book yer gonna buy,' asked Kevin.

'Dunno, don't really read books.'

Zed asked Kevin why he hadn't bought anything in. Kevin laughed. 'Like what, never went anywhere, I was stuck in this dump for six weeks.'

Zed was quiet for a moment. 'You could come with me next time.'

'Where' asked Kevin.'

To Tim and Peggy's on the canal, would yer mum let yer come? '

'Spect so, she'd be glad to get rid of me.'

Zed told Kevin that he was hoping to go down at Easter and he would ask Peggy when she next rang.

'Yeah,' said Kevin punching Zed on the arm.

'That'll be cool, ain't never stayed away before.'

It was a warm afternoon so instead of going straight home they took a longer route through the park that ran alongside the river. After chasing each other across the wooden benches that encircled the flower garden, they sat exhausted on the end of Cherry Garden Pier talking excitedly of the adventures they would both have on the waterways next Easter with Tim, Peggy and Barney.

See you on our next adventure!

GLOSSARY OF TERMS

ABSEILING: Performing a controlled descent on a rope down a vertical surface such as a rock face, a climbing wall or a tall building.

TO GO ASTERN: To go backwards on a boat.

AQUEDUCT: A bridge, usually with several arches, carrying a water-filled channel, such as a canal or river, over a road, river or valley.

BACK SPLICING: A method of weaving the strands of a rope back in on themselves in order to prevent fraying.

BILGES: The lowest compartments of the boat, beneath the water line.

BLOOD KNOT: A favourite knot for fishermen, used to join lines of similar size.

BOLLARD: A post made of wood, iron, or stone on a bank or quay, for mooring a boat to.

BOW: The front end of the boat, pronounced to rhyme with 'now'.

BOW LINE: The rope on the front of the boat.

BUCKBY CAN: A traditional design of water can, often decorated with roses and castles, used by families on the old working boats.

BUCKET-&-CHUCKIT: A basic toilet consisting of a small metal bin (the 'bucket') with a wooden seat, that would have to be emptied when full ('chuckit').

BUOYANCY AID: A zip-up jacket to keep you afloat in the water.

BUTTY: A narrowboat without an engine, which is towed by a motor boat with an engine, either alongside or behind.

TO CAST OFF: To untie the lines from the mooring and get under way.

CHAMBER: The watertight enclosure between the top and bottom gates of a lock.

CLEAT: A metal T-shape on the bow of the boat or on a jetty to tie the mooring lines around.

CLUB HAMMER: A large, heavy hammer used for driving mooring spikes into the ground.

CUT: Another name for the canal, reflecting the fact that it was 'cut' out of the ground by the Navvies.

FENDERS: Protective buffers, usually cylinders made of plastic or rope, these are hung on the side of boats to protect them from damage when banging against lock sides and gates, banks or other boats. Larger fenders of various shapes are hung at the bow or stern of boats to protect them from bumps.

FID: A conical shaped tool made of wood, used in splicing rope.

GALLEY: The name of the kitchen on a boat.

GUNWALE: (Pronounced 'gunnel') The narrow ledge running down the side of the boat along which you can walk from the front (bow) to the back (stern).

GUY STRAPS: The rubber bands that keep the canvas attached to the cleats on the side of the boat.

HATCHES: Openings in the boat, either hinged vertical doorways in the sides or sliding horizontal hatches in the roof. Can also be used as emergency exits.

HEADS: The name for the toilets on a boat.

HULL: The bottom of the boat.

HURRICANE LAMP: An oil or paraffin lamp with glass sides to prevent the flame from being blown out in the wind.

JETTY A wooden, metal, or concrete platform that a boat can moor alongside.

KEEL HAULING: The practice of dragging a person underwater from one side of a ship to another, used many years ago by the Royal Navy as a most unpleasant punishment.

LEGGING: The method of moving horse-drawn, engine-less boats through tunnels by lying on planks across the roof and 'walking' against the sides of the tunnel. The horse would be led over the top of the tunnel to meet the boat on the other side.

LOCKS: Water-filled chambers with gates which can be opened and closed to let boats through. At either end of the chamber are paddles which can be opened and closed to let water through to raise and lower water levels in the chamber, enabling boats to be carried between stretches of water of different levels, i.e. when going up and down hills.

TO MOOR: To stop alongside the canal bank or a wharf.

MOORING SPIKES: Spiked metal stakes which are banged into the canal bank with a club   hammer, to tie to when mooring.

NAVVIES: Short for 'navigators', the labourers who dug the canals or 'navigations' using just shovels and pickaxes.

OUTLET: A place where water runs into the canal from a building or stream.

PADDLE: A sliding gate which when lifted allows water to either enter the chamber of a lock from the upper pound, raising the level in the chamber, or to flow out of the chamber into the lower pound, lowering the level in the chamber.

POUND: The level stretch of water between two locks.

PROPELLER: A revolving shaft with spiral blades that causes a boat to move (i.e. 'propels' it) by spinning round and creating a backward thrust of water .

RAFTED UP: A term to describe kayaks all joined

together in a line, with each paddler holding onto the cockpit of the kayak next to them.

ROSES AND CASTLES: The popular name for the traditional paintwork of narrowboats.

RUDDER: The means of steering a boat, this is a large vertical pivoting blade mounted under the water at the stern of the boat, controlled by the tiller bar or sometimes by a wheel.

STERN: The back end of the boat.

STERN GLAND: The area around the propeller shaft at the point where it exits a boat's hull underwater is packed with wadding and watertight grease. This is the most common method of preventing water from entering the hull while still allowing the propeller shaft to turn. The grease is 'topped up' after each journey by turning a screw on a grease-packed piston.

STERN LINE: The rope at the back or stern of the boat.

TIE OFF: Secure the boat by its lines to a bollard or cleat.

TILLER: The brass bar used for steering the boat. To move the boat left, the tiller is moved to the right, and vice versa.

TOWPATH: The path next to the canal from which horses once towed boats before they had engines.

TOW ROPE: The rope used to tow the butty along behind the boat with the engine.

VIADUCT: A bridge usually composed of several small spans, built to carry a road or railway over a valley.

WASH / WAKE: The v-shaped wave set up by a boat travelling fast, which will rock other boats it passes, particularly in shallow water.

WEED HATCH: A hatch at the stern of the boat to access the propeller in order to remove weeds and plastic bags which can get would round it, preventing the propeller from turning.

WHARF: A landing place or pier where boats can tie up to load or unload.

WINDING HOLE: A wider area of canal where even the longest boats can turn. Pronounced as in 'the west wind', not 'winding a watch'.

WINDLASS: Also known as a lock handle or key, this is a metal handle used to wind open the paddles on a lock.